CHANGE
OF HEART

CHANGE OF HEART

A ROBYN HUNTER MYSTERY

NORAH McCLINTOCK

MINNEAPOLIS

Darby Creek
A division of Lerner Publishing Group, Inc.
241 First Avenue North
Minneapolis, MN 55401 U.S.A.

Website address: www.lernerbooks.com

The image in this book is used with the permission of: Front
cover: © Jonathan Daniel/Getty Images.

Main body text set in Janson Text Lt Std 11.5/15.
Typeface provided by Linotype AG.

Library of Congress Cataloging-in-Publication Data

McClintock, Norah.
    Change of heart / Norah McClintock. — 1st U.S. ed.
        p.   cm. — (Robyn Hunter mysteries ; #7)
    ISBN 978–0–7613–8317–8 (lib. bdg. : alk. paper)
        [1. Mystery and detective stories. 2. Murder—Fiction.
    3. Dating (Social customs)—Fiction.] I. Title.
    PZ7.M478414184Ch 2013
    [Fic]—dc23   2012017535

Manufactured in the United States of America
1 – BP – 12/31/12

To all good friends

CHAPTER **ONE**

I wish I could say that I was surprised when I stepped out of school and directly into a full-blown fight, but I wasn't, even though this particular fight involved my best friend Billy Royal, who is normally the sweetest, gentlest person in the world. He literally wouldn't hurt a fly. Whenever anyone gives him a hard time, he walks away—not because he's afraid, but because he believes that violence doesn't solve anything. But there he was.

For someone who looks like a beanpole, Billy is in pretty good shape. He runs regularly. He kickboxes a couple of times a week—for the exercise. He plays pick-up hockey whenever he can. He could probably hold his own against a lot of guys if he had to. Unfortunately, the person he was locked in combat with was Sean Sloane. I had no idea who had started it, but I had a pretty good idea what it was about.

Sean was all muscle. He was tall like Billy, toned—I never saw a guy look better in jeans than Sean Sloane—and extremely physical. He was a hockey star, captain of one of the best teams in the area. In the regional league, anyway. Major junior was the highest level of play, Morgan explained, but playing regional league kept Sean eligible to compete on college teams in the U.S.

Oh yeah: two weeks ago Sean had started going out with my other best friend, Morgan Turner, who up until then had been going out with Billy. It's complicated.

I had stepped outside just in time to see Billy shove Sean—hard. His palms slammed into Sean's chest and sent Sean reeling backwards. Billy went after him again, his hands curled into fists. I had never seen Billy's face so twisted with rage.

That's when Morgan shouted, "Stop it, Billy," which surprised me. She was looking at Billy as if he were the one who had started the fight. She grabbed his arm and tried to pull him away from Sean, but Billy shook her off. He and Sean circled each other like prizefighters.

"Billy!" Morgan shouted.

But Billy wasn't listening. I don't think he was aware of anyone or anything except Sean.

A crowd gathered. I recognized Tamara Sanders, who had been Sean's girlfriend until he started going out with Morgan. She was watching the goings-on with obvious amusement. I don't know if she thought Billy could actually win, but I bet she would have shaken his hand if he had. Half a dozen guys had formed a loose semicircle behind Sean—all jocks like him.

"Jon, do something," Morgan said to one of them.

Jon Czerny was on the same hockey team as Sean. He was taller and beefier than Sean and looked like the kind of guy who could do a lot of damage if he wanted to. He could also probably break up a fight—if he wanted to. But he didn't make a move to intervene. Neither did any of the other jocks. Like Tamara, they seemed to be enjoying the fight.

Morgan looked around wildly. She spotted someone out on the football field.

"Colin!" she called. "Colin!"

Colin Sloane was Sean's brother. When Morgan called him, his head bobbed up, his face brightened, and he immediately started to jog over to where she was standing. Because of the crowd that had gathered around Sean and Billy, I don't think he realized what was happening.

Standing farther back from the fray was Dennis Hanson. Dennis was, as Billy diplomatically put it, different. He was brilliant at math and had a reputation as a chess master. But he rarely made eye contact with anyone and was widely regarded as, well, weird. I heard someone say he had Asperger's Syndrome, but I don't know if that was true or not. Even if it was, it didn't stop a lot of kids from making fun of him. Most people avoided him entirely. But not Billy. He accepted Dennis the way he was, quirks and all.

Now Dennis's eyes were riveted on Billy. It was the first time I'd seen him look directly at another human being. I couldn't tell, though, whether he was afraid for Billy or thrilled that Billy was taking on someone like Sean.

Next to Dennis—but not too close, no one ever got too close to Dennis—was Aaron Arthurs, rumored to be one of the other smartest kids in school. He was a real techhead. I had been in the same computer class as Aaron last year. He knew far more than the teacher, who never hesitated to call on him for help and who told us all, repeatedly, "Mark my words, people, Aaron is going to be the next Steve Jobs." In other words, he was a total geek. It didn't help that his mom was one of the school secretaries—and that she was super strict. If I'd been Aaron, I would have transferred.

Worse, Aaron was often found in the school office after hours, helping his mom tidy up before they went home together, and the principal had called him in more than once to troubleshoot computer problems. Aaron was watching the fight with the same rapt expression as Dennis. Unlike Dennis, he was smiling. He was probably hoping to see Sean take a public beating.

But that's not what happened.

Instead, Sean landed a punch—it looked like a good one—right on Billy's nose. Billy's head snapped back. Blood gushed into his mouth and down his chin. He stared in astonishment at Sean, and I thought, *That's it, fight's over*. Sean must have thought so, too, because he smiled at Morgan. Billy pivoted around. I think he wanted to see Morgan's reaction. As soon as his back was turned, Sean rushed him.

"Billy, look out!" I shouted.

That's when Morgan noticed me standing there.

Billy spun back to face Sean. One of his long legs snapped out in a karate kick. It connected with Sean in what for guys is a very sensitive spot. Sean sank to his knees groaning just as his brother Colin broke through the crowd.

"Sean." Colin rushed to his brother's side. "Are you okay?"

Mr. Dormer, one of the vice principals, pushed through the crowd and frowned in disapproval. "Sloane, are you hurt?"

"I'll be okay," Sean said through clenched teeth. His face was red. I would have bet anything that his embarrassment rivaled whatever pain he was feeling. While Colin helped him to his feet, Sean scowled at the crowd around him, daring anyone to snicker. Someone did: Dennis Hanson.

"What are you laughing at, freak?" Sean snarled. "You want to see what this feels like?"

"Leave him alone," Billy said, his voice muffled by the sleeve of his jacket, which he had pressed against his nose to try to stop the bleeding. "He didn't mean anything." He glanced at Dennis, who was staring resolutely at the ground.

"What about you, Royal?" Mr. Dormer said to Billy. He pulled Billy's hand away from his nose. "Is it broken?"

"I don't know," Billy said.

Mr. Dormer did a slow scan of spectators' faces and picked Aaron out of the crowd. "Take Royal inside," he said. "Have your mother call his parents. You'll need to have someone look at that nose, Royal."

Billy nodded miserably.

"You go, too, Sloane," Mr. Dormer said. "Report to the office. Wait for me there."

Sean limped to the door, supported by Colin. Billy—always a gentleman, even when he was bleeding—opened it for them. Maybe he was sorry for hurting Sean. But Sean didn't seem remotely sorry for hurting Billy, and Colin glowered at him as he muscled his way into the school. If Mr. Dormer hadn't been standing right there, he probably would have taken a swing at Billy.

Mr. Dormer looked around at the crowd.

"Who started this?" he said.

Morgan stepped forward.

"Billy did."

Billy turned and looked mournfully at her before stepping inside.

"Billy attacked Sean," Morgan said.

Attacked? Billy? Mr. Dormer must have been thinking the same thing that I was—*Impossible!*

"Billy Royal attacked Sean Sloane?" he said. "Why would he do that?"

"Because he's jealous," Morgan said. "He doesn't like that I'm going out with Sean."

"I see," Mr. Dormer said. "And you saw what happened?"

"Yes. I was walking with Sean. All of a sudden Billy grabbed him. When Sean tried to walk away, Billy shoved him."

Mr. Dormer blinked and shook his head as if he had woken up to find himself in a parallel universe. In the world he normally inhabited, people like Billy Royal did not instigate fights with people like Sean Sloane.

"Even after Billy shoved him, Sean still tried to walk away," Morgan said. "That's when Billy attacked him."

"But Billy's the one who's bleeding," I pointed out.

Mr. Dormer gave me a sour look. The message was clear: he was talking to Morgan, not to me.

"Sean was just defending himself," Morgan said.

Mr. Dormer shook his head again. He thanked Morgan and turned to go back inside, presumably to his office, presumably to sort things out and punish whoever was to blame, which, if he accepted Morgan's version of the events, was going to be Billy.

"Are you sure you're not exaggerating?" I said after he had gone. "I mean, when was the last time Billy attacked anyone?"

"Are you calling me a liar?" Morgan said.

"No. But this is Billy we're talking about."

"Billy's lucky that all Sean did was defend himself," Morgan said. "If Sean had wanted to, he could have really hurt Billy. But he didn't. He's not like that." I thought about Sean jumping Billy from behind. That had nothing to do with self-defense. It was dirty fighting, plain and simple.

By the end of the school day, everyone knew that Billy had been given a three-day suspension for "attacking" Sean.

"Poor Billy," I said when I met Morgan at her locker after school.

Morgan slammed her locker door.

"Why do you always take his side?" she said.

"I'm trying not to take sides. You and Billy are my friends."

"You're such a hypocrite, Robyn."

"What?"

"I know what you think," she said. "You think I shouldn't have broken up with Billy. But look at you. You broke up with Ben."

It was true. I had broken up with Ben Logan. I'd told myself that it wasn't right to keep going out with him when it was obvious that he cared for me a lot more than I cared for him. And when I was spending most of my time wishing that he was someone else: Nick D'Angelo, who I had been going out with before I met Ben and . . . well, it was complicated.

Ben didn't take the breakup well. But he and I didn't go to the same school, so he didn't have to see me every day. I think that made it easier for him than breaking up with Morgan was for Billy.

"If you don't want to go out with Billy anymore, that's your business," I said. "But he's still my friend. And he's devastated." He really was. Instead of being his usual easygoing and cheery self, he had become sullen and withdrawn. Whenever he saw me with Morgan, he veered off in another direction. He hadn't come right out and said so—after all, he's a guy—but I was pretty sure that he thought I supported Morgan's decision to dump him. That I was on her side. But I wasn't. "I feel sorry for him, that's all. I still don't understand what happened between you two. What did Billy do that was so terrible?"

"There you go again, defending him."

"I asked a question. Since when does that constitute defending someone?"

"It's the way you asked, like you can't believe that Billy would ever do anything terrible. Like he's perfect and I'm the one who always messes up."

"I didn't say that—"

"It's chemistry, Robyn. Sean and I have chemistry."

"I thought you had chemistry with Billy." That's what she had told me dozens, maybe hundreds, of times.

"Well, I have better chemistry with Sean. And don't give me that look again. This is not my fault. It just happened."

"You make it sound like a car accident," I said. Was that how it worked: one minute you were going merrily on your way and the next, out of the blue, your heart collided with someone else's and there was nothing you could do about it? But that wasn't what had happened between Morgan and Billy. That had been a slow build-up over years. Maybe that was her point. Maybe that was why she and Billy hadn't lasted.

Or was it something else?

"Are you saying you never really loved Billy?" I asked.

"No," she said. "At least, I don't think that's what I'm saying. But come on, Robyn. You didn't think Billy and I were going to be together forever, did you?"

To be honest, I had never thought about it. But now that she mentioned it, I suppose that was exactly the picture I'd had in my mind. They'd been such a perfect couple. Billy brought out the best in Morgan, and Morgan made Billy smile almost all the time.

"I hate to say it, Robyn, but in a way I'm glad Billy attacked Sean . . ."

"What?"

She hesitated for a moment.

"I didn't tell you this because I know how you feel about Billy," she said slowly. "But he's been acting really weird. He calls my phone fifteen or twenty times a day. He follows me around, even when I'm with Sean—especially when I'm with Sean. He's practically stalking me."

"Billy?" I said. "Billy would never—"

"You're doing it again. I'm not lying, Robyn. And I'm not exaggerating. He's driving me crazy. Now that he's suspended, maybe he'll stop harassing me. Maybe he'll give up and get over it."

. . .

I went to Billy's house after school. I rang the doorbell a dozen times, but there was no answer. I wondered if his mom had taken him to the hospital. I wondered if his nose was broken after all. I dug out my cell phone and ended up in his voice mail. Then I headed for my father's place.

My parents are divorced. I mostly live with my mother, but I spend every other weekend at my father's. Sometimes when my mom, who is a lawyer, is working on a big case and puts in long nights at her office, I stay at my dad's place during the week, too. Most of the time he's glad to have me.

My first clue that this was not one of those times: when my dad heard me come through his front door, he popped his head out of his office (one of the few truly closed-in rooms in his open-concept loft) and looked not-so-pleasantly surprised to see me.

"Robbie," he said. "I wasn't expecting you."

No kidding. He seemed flustered, and my father isn't someone who is easily flustered.

"You want me to leave, Dad?"

My second clue that I wasn't being welcomed with open arms: my dad didn't immediately say, *No, of course not*. He seemed to be thinking it over.

"What's the matter?" I said.

He glanced back over his shoulder. That's when I realized that there was someone else in his office with him. My first thought was, *It's a woman*. After three years of being separated and one year of being divorced, my mom had accepted a marriage proposal from a man named Ted Gold. Maybe my dad had finally taken the hint. Maybe he was moving on.

But, no, that wasn't it.

"Nick is here," he said.

Nick stepped into the doorway beside my dad, and my heart slammed to a stop. I hadn't seen Nick in a while. He used to rent an apartment on the second floor of the building my dad owns. My dad occupies the entire third floor. A gourmet restaurant leases the ground floor. But Nick had abandoned his apartment a few months ago. He had taken off without any warning. He had reappeared only a few weeks ago, also without warning. The whole time he was gone, I'd waited to hear from him. I had also started going out with Ben. Now Ben was history, but Nick didn't know that yet. Up until this very minute I'd had no idea where he was. And the last time I'd seen him, he'd told me that it was probably best if we both moved on.

And yet here he was, standing beside my father. Nick's jet-black hair was longish and scruffy. A jagged scar cut across his cheek, from the bridge of his nose to his right ear. He was dressed, as usual, head to toe in black. When he looked at me with his amethyst-colored eyes, he took my breath away. He always did. Had he come looking for me?

"Nick," I said. "What are you doing here?"

I didn't mean it the way Nick obviously took it. His whole body stiffened. He turned to my father. "I'd better get to work. It'll take a little time, okay, Mac?"

Mac? Nick always used to call my father Mr. Hunter.

"No problem," my father said. "And don't forget Thursday night. You know where we're supposed to be, right?"

We? What was going on?

Nick nodded. He barely glanced at me as he strode out of my dad's office, through the enormous living space, to the front door where I stood frozen by surprise and longing. When he got close, I had to fight the urge to reach out and touch him. He nodded curtly at me as he passed but didn't say a word. The door clicked shut behind me, and I heard footsteps—boot steps—going down the stairs.

"What was he doing here?" I said.

"It's a personal matter, Robbie."

"Is he all right?" Nick had been in plenty of trouble in his life, a lot of it involving the law. Most of the time he tried to do the right thing, but not all the time.

"As far as I can tell," my father said.

"What did he want?"

"I told you, Robbie. It's personal."

"What are you two doing on Thursday night?"

"I can't tell you that."

My father used to be a police officer. He was always good at keeping secrets or, as he put it, not discussing official police matters with civilians, which included me. Now that he's retired from the police and has his own private security business, he's even better at keeping secrets. I could threaten, I could argue, I could cry, but all I would get is, "Sorry, Robbie. No can do."

I hovered near the door, torn between staying and going. Nick's footsteps grew fainter until I heard nothing at all. I dropped my backpack to the floor, kicked off my boots, and headed for my dad's guest room, which doubles as my bedroom. I didn't slam the door, but I did close it firmly behind me.

It took longer than I expected—a full ten minutes—before my father knocked.

"Come on, Robbie," he said from the other side of the door. "You're not mad at me, are you?"

I was. But I got up off the bed and opened the door anyway.

"He's not in trouble, if that's what's bothering you," my dad said.

It wasn't.

"Did he ask about me?"

My dad looked me directly in the eye. He shook his head. "I'm sorry, Robbie."

So was I.

"I have to run out and get some groceries," my dad said. "You want to help me make dinner?"

I said okay, even though food was the last thing on my mind.

My dad shopped. We cooked. We ate. We cleaned up. Then Morgan called.

"You have to do something for me," she said. "You have to talk to Billy. You have to make him stop."

CHAPTER **TWO**

"Do you want me to wait for you?" my dad said. We were sitting in his Porsche at the curb outside of Billy's house.

I shook my head.

"I don't know how long I'm going to be," I said. "I'll just go home after." My mom's house was only a couple of blocks from Billy's. My dad lived much farther away.

My dad said okay. He probably thought I was still mad at him, but I wasn't. I was mad at Nick. Like I said, it was complicated.

I kissed my dad on the cheek to show him there were no hard feelings. After he drove away, I rang Billy's doorbell.

Billy's mother answered.

"He's upstairs," she said. She meant the third-floor family room, where I found Billy slumped in front of the TV, his cell phone in one hand, the remote in the other, a

15

damp cloth in a bowl of melting ice on his lap, and what looked like a history essay beside him on the couch. Both of his eyes were black, and his nose was swollen. He didn't even glance at me when I entered the room.

"Hey, Billy," I said. "Are you okay? How's your nose? Is it broken?"

No answer.

"I called you," I said. "Didn't you get my message?"

Nothing.

"Come on, Billy. Talk to me."

Instead, all I got was stony silence. He reminded me of Nick—which was weird because Billy is nothing like Nick. I crossed the room and shut off the TV. Billy clicked it back on. I stood in front of the screen to block his view.

"Leave me alone, Robyn," he said.

"No way. You're my friend."

"He stole her from me."

I turned off the TV again, pried the remote from his hand, and sat down beside him.

"She likes him, Billy. I know it hurts, and I'm really sorry." I had told him that dozens of times already. "But you're making yourself crazy. You have to try to get over it."

"But I love her."

I knew how that felt. There's nothing worse than wanting to be with someone who doesn't want to be with you.

"Billy, the more you harass her, the worse you make it."

"Harass her?" He looked hurt and confused.

"Morgan called me—"

"She said I was harassing her?"

"She says you've been phoning her nonstop. She says you follow her around. Billy, you attacked Sean."

He hung his head.

"I know it was wrong," he said. "I knew it even while I was doing it. But he gave me this look. And he said—" He broke off abruptly.

"He said what?"

"It doesn't matter." His eyes glistened when he looked back up at me. "I couldn't help it, Robyn. I lost my temper." I tried to remember the last time that had happened. Billy was good-natured, laid-back. I didn't think he *had* a temper. "I don't know what to do. I can't stop thinking about her. I just want to talk to her. But she won't take my calls. She won't even speak to me."

"She wants you to leave her alone."

"What am I going to do?"

I touched his arm. "Come on, Billy. You know Morgan. You know how she is once she makes up her mind about something. There's nothing you can do."

I stayed for another hour and listened while Billy told me—again—about finding Morgan and Sean together that first time ("He was kissing her, Robyn, and he saw me. He looked right at me and he kept right on kissing her") and about confronting Morgan ("She said, 'I should have told you.' You know what that means, right, Robyn? It means she was seeing him while we were still together."). He told me that all he wanted, all he had ever wanted, was to talk to her.

"If I could just explain to her how I feel—"

"Billy, it doesn't make any difference how you feel. Not about this." I'd told him that over and over again, but he didn't listen. Not that I blamed him. I understood his pain and confusion a whole lot better than I understood why Morgan had dumped him.

"But I love her," he said—again.

I sighed.

"You got suspended for three days, Billy. That's big trouble. The next step is getting expelled. You don't want that to happen, do you?"

He looked at me with liquid eyes. Finally he shook his head.

When I got up to leave, he said, "Is Dennis okay?"

"What?"

"Dennis. Sean didn't hassle him after I left, did he?"

"I don't think so."

"Well, he'd better not," Billy said fiercely. "Dennis is different, but he's not stupid. He's a good guy. He's out every single morning during migration season, picking up birds. He's smart, too. Way smarter than Sean. Even the professors are impressed by how much Dennis knows about birds." He meant the two university professors who supported DARC, the Downtown Avian Rescue Club that Billy had founded. The club helped save injured migratory birds. According to Billy, Dennis was one of its most enthusiastic members.

"I don't think Sean would ever do anything to Dennis," I said. "He was just in pain."

Billy looked doubtful. "Sean Sloane isn't what Morgan thinks, Robyn," he said. "He may be a good hockey player, but that doesn't make him a good guy. You should tell Morgan—"

I was tired of being in the middle. Morgan and Billy were my oldest and closest friends, but we never hung around together anymore, and I was always worrying what one of them would think if I was spotted with the other one.

"It's Morgan's life," I said. "I'm not telling her anything." I glanced at the essay on the couch beside him. "You want me to hand that in for you?"

He just shrugged. I reached across him, picked up the essay, and read the first paragraph.

"I'll put it in Ms. Carver's box for you." No response. "And I'll bring you your homework assignments tomorrow, okay?" Nothing. "Billy?"

"Okay," he said finally.

. . .

Morgan was waiting for me outside school the next morning.

"Did you talk to him?" she said.

I nodded.

"And? Is he going to leave me alone?"

"I don't know."

"Why is everyone making this so hard for us?"

"Everyone?"

"Billy is harassing me. Tamara is harassing Sean."

"She is?"

"She thinks she's a big deal because she hosts that lame teen show on TV," Morgan said. "Now she's after him to do some stupid documentary. If you ask me, she's just trying to get him back. But it's not going to work." She looked defiantly at me. Then she said, "You really should get to know him, Robyn. You'd like him."

Like everyone else in my school, I knew *of* Sean. But I didn't actually know him. He was a senior, so he wasn't in any of my classes, and, to be honest, after Morgan started going out with him I had no interest in getting acquainted. Billy would have been so hurt if he'd seen me hanging out with Morgan and Sean. But Billy wasn't going to be at school for the next couple of days, and I was kind of curious to find out more about the guy who had stolen Morgan's heart.

"Come on," Morgan said, looping her arm through mine. "I'll introduce you. You'll see what I mean."

We trooped into school and up the stairs to the second floor, where Sean's locker was. It was hard to miss. Someone—not Sean, according to Morgan—had pasted a big gold star decorated with a hockey stick and a puck to the front of it. So far no one—not the janitorial staff, not the school administration, not even surly Mr. Dormer—had removed it, even though decorating the outside of locker doors was strictly against the rules.

Morgan came to an abrupt stop as soon as we rounded the corner. A crowd had gathered around the locker. Morgan stared at it for a moment before rushing to Sean's side.

"What happened?" she said.

My first guess, as I elbowed my way through the crowd, was that both a tornado and a paper shredder had slammed into his locker. The locker door was open, and the floor in front of it was covered with ripped and crumpled paper.

"Someone tore up all my notes," Sean said. "And a major assignment that I was supposed to hand in today. And look." He bent down and picked up a flash drive—well, what had been a flash drive. It looked as if someone had stomped on it with construction boots. "Every assignment I've ever done was on there."

"What's going on here?" said a stern voice. Mr. Dormer. He had a knack for showing up where the action was.

Sean said that he had arrived at school to find that the lock had been cut off his locker—he showed it to Mr. Dormer—and that everything inside, except his textbooks, had been torn to shreds.

"Even the picture of my girlfriend," he said, slipping an arm around Morgan, who went from looking indignant on his behalf to looking as if she were about to melt.

"But you have everything backed up on your computer at home, right, Sean?" she said.

Sean shook his head.

"My brothers and I share the computer." Sean had two older brothers—Colin, who was still in school, and Kevin, who had graduated two years ago. "They're always fooling with my stuff, so I don't keep anything important on the hard drive." He turned and sought out someone in the crowd—Colin. "Isn't that right?"

Colin looked down at the floor for a moment. "Yeah," he said. "That's right."

"All my assignments were on here." Sean held out the mangled flash drive. "And now they're gone."

"Do you have any idea who might have done this?" Mr. Dormer said.

Morgan avoided my eyes as she said, "I do."

She and Sean followed Mr. Dormer to the office.

. . .

I caught up with Morgan in the library at lunchtime. There was a stack of books on the table in front of her. It looked like she was researching a biology assignment, but that didn't make sense. She wasn't taking biology this year.

"Why did you do that?" I said.

"Why did I do what?"

"Why did you tell Mr. Dormer that Billy vandalized Sean's locker? You don't know it was him. Besides, he's suspended. He's not even at school today."

"Then how come the head janitor saw him here at seven thirty this morning?" Morgan said.

"He did?"

"Mr. Dormer checked with all the staff to see if anyone had seen anything. The head janitor saw Billy going down the stairs to one of the back exits."

"He's sure it was Billy?"

Morgan nodded grimly.

"Did he see Billy vandalize Sean's locker?"

"No. But who else could it have been, Robyn? You saw the fight yesterday. And look at this." She produced a crumpled envelope from her purse and handed it to me. "Go ahead. Open it."

I pulled a sheet of paper from the envelope. It was a letter from Billy.

"When did he send this?"

"He didn't send it. He left it in my locker this morning, probably right before he trashed Sean's locker."

"Are you sure?"

"It wasn't there yesterday when I left school," Morgan said. "Sean has been getting phone calls, too. Someone has been calling him night and day. When he answers, all he hears is breathing. When he doesn't answer, the caller leaves a message telling him he's going to be sorry."

"The caller? Are you saying it's Billy?"

"Of course it's Billy," Morgan said.

"You've heard his voice? You know for a fact it's him?"

"The person always calls from a number that's listed as private. Sean tried calling back, but he couldn't get through. And the voice sounds weird, like, scrambled.

But I know it's Billy. Who else would it be? And now he's trashed Sean's locker and wrecked all of Sean's notes. He destroyed a bio project that Sean was supposed to hand in today." I glanced at the stack of books in front of Morgan. "His teacher is giving him an extension. I'm helping him get it done."

Sean was a lucky guy. Morgan is a straight-A student.

"Billy better stop acting like a psycho," Morgan said. "If he doesn't, he's going to end up in serious trouble."

.   .   .

I was on my way out of school when I remembered Billy's history essay. I dashed back to the office. The place was deserted except for Ms. Arthurs, who was on the phone. She glanced at me. I told her I wanted to hand something in to Ms. Carver.

"You can put it in her mailbox," she said, putting one hand over the phone's mouthpiece and waving at the door that led to the copy room where the teachers' mailboxes were. She went back to her phone call.

I pushed open the door, startling the room's only occupant. Aaron Arthurs was standing at the photocopier. He spun around when I walked in.

"What are you doing in here?" he said.

"I'm dropping off something," I said, not that it was any of his business. "Your mom said it was okay." I scanned the mailboxes for Ms. Carver's name. "What are you doing?"

He gave me a look like he thought I was brain-dead for asking. He was making a copy—obviously. I could see some sheets in the photocopier's output tray and tried to see what they were. Aaron stepped in front of it, blocking my view. Whatever. I found Ms Carver's mailbox and slipped Billy's essay into it.

Then I went to his house and rang the doorbell, but no one answered. I tried to call Billy. Still no answer. I slid his assignments through the mail slot and went home.

.   .   .

Billy wasn't making things easy on himself. He was standing outside school when I got off the bus the next morning. His hair was disheveled. His eyes were swollen and bruised. The rest of his face was pale. He looked like he'd been up all night.

"Did you get the homework assignments I left you?" I said.

He didn't even look at me. Instead, he looked up the street. I was willing to bet he was watching for Morgan.

"Billy—" I touched his arm.

Then, boom, just like that, Sean appeared. He grabbed Billy and spun him around.

"Stay away from her, you got that?" he said. "Stay away from her and stay away from me."

Billy just stared at him. Colin stood beside Sean, ready to back him up—not that Sean needed backup.

Like Sean, Colin also played hockey, but everyone said he wasn't as good. I'd heard that he'd suffered a couple of concussions on the ice. He hadn't graduated yet, even though he was older than Sean.

"You hear me?" Sean said. He had the front of Billy's jacket bunched up in his fists while he talked. Kids passing us on the way into school stopped to watch what was going on. "Do you hear what I'm telling you?"

"Leave him alone," I said to Sean. Okay, so maybe he was Morgan's boyfriend and maybe Morgan was one of my best friends, but so was Billy—even if he was acting like a lunatic.

"This creep is stalking my girlfriend," Sean said, barely glancing at me. Billy flinched at the accusation.

"He spied on her while she was at my house last night," he said. He turned to Billy. "I know you were there. There were footprints outside the den window. You were watching us, and then you followed her home. Right, Colin?" Colin nodded. "Colin saw you watching us," Sean said. "He followed you."

I glanced at Billy. His face turned red.

"Stay away from Morgan and stay away from me," Sean said again, "or you'll be sorry. I know where you live, Royal." He shoved Billy backward and then stalked off. Colin followed him. The kids who had been watching and listening all stared at Billy. But when nothing else happened, they quickly lost interest.

"Is it true, Billy?" I said when we were alone again. "Were you spying on Morgan and Sean?"

Billy's nod was almost imperceptible.

I sighed. "Go home, Billy, before you get into any more trouble."

I didn't go into the school until he turned and walked away.

. . .

"Come to the game tonight," Morgan said when she found me at my locker a few minutes later. Her perkiness told me that she hadn't heard about what had just happened, and I didn't want to be the one to tell her.

"I don't know," I said.

"We'll all go out afterwards. I want you to get to know Sean. You'll like him. I know you will."

After what I had just witnessed, I wasn't so sure.

"I have a ton of homework," I said. It happened to be true. But mostly I felt it would be disloyal to Billy.

"This is important to me, Robyn," Morgan said. "I like him, and you're my best friend. Please?"

"Well—"

Morgan beamed. "I'll meet you at the arena at eight o'clock. We'll have great seats. It'll be fun. You'll see."

She was wrong. It turned out to be no fun at all.

CHAPTER **THREE**

Not only was Sean captain of the hottest hockey team in his league, he was also the league's leading scorer. Morgan told me that he had already been scouted by several colleges. Apparently the word among hockey fans was that Sean was destined for the big leagues. So it came as no surprise, as the regional playoffs began, that the arena was jammed.

Morgan had told me to meet her at the team entrance at the back of the arena. As I rounded the corner of the building, I spotted Sean talking to a girl who had her back to me.

"Come on, Sean," she was saying. "I made a pitch and they loved it. I told them you agreed. I said it was a go."

"That's not my problem, Tamara," Sean said.

Tamara Sanders, Sean's ex-girlfriend.

"But this is important to me," Tamara said. "And the exposure would be great for you. Give me a break. If I have to tell them you've pulled out, I'm going to look like an idiot."

"So?" Sean said. "That's your problem. And after what you did—"

"Come on, Sean. I said I was sorry. And you promised."

"Things have changed." Sean pushed open the door and went inside. Tamara scowled when she saw me.

"What are you staring at?" she said. She stormed past me, muttering under her breath, and almost collided with Morgan, who'd come around the corner looking for me. Morgan smiled smugly like the victor she considered herself to be.

"What was she doing here?" she asked.

"She was talking to Sean about something."

That wiped the smile off Morgan's face. "About what?"

"I think it was something about that documentary you said she wants to do on Sean."

"And?"

"And nothing. Sean told her he wasn't interested."

Morgan perked up when she heard that.

"Good," she said. "Come on." She pushed open the team entrance. We stepped inside and were immediately blocked by a grizzled old man wearing khaki work pants and a heavy plaid shirt.

"This door is for players only," he began. Then he squinted at Morgan. "Oh, it's you." He broke into an appreciative smile—Morgan has that effect on guys, even old ones.

"Hi, Wayne," Morgan said breezily. "This is my friend Robyn."

Wayne nodded curtly at me.

"The guys are in the locker room, and that's off-limits," she said as she led me down a long corridor. "We'll catch up with Sean after the game. I can't wait to introduce you." Her eyes gleamed with excitement. I remembered when her eyes used to sparkle like that at the thought of seeing Billy, and I felt sorry for him all over again.

I hadn't been inside the arena since elementary school, when I had taken skating lessons. The place sure looked different now. It was cleaner, less run-down. And it looked as if more improvements were planned. Scaffolding and construction materials were piled along one of the outer walls. But the people bustling in, pulling off hats and scarves and gloves, didn't seem to care. Morgan was right about how good our seats were. We were in the first row, right near the center. Colin and Kevin Sloane had the seats next to us.

While we waited for the game to begin, Morgan talked nonstop about Sean—how much fun he was, what a great hockey player he was, how smart he was, how his mom insisted that he keep up his grades in addition to playing hockey.

"That's why he's planning on going to college, even though he's good enough to go pro," Morgan said with obvious approval. "His mom made him promise that he would get an education. She doesn't want him to be another dumb jock with nothing to fall back on if hockey doesn't work out for him."

I glanced at Sean's brothers. Colin was still trying to get enough credits to graduate. And Morgan had told me that Kevin had barely made it through high school. He was an assistant coach with a junior hockey team and worked part-time as a mechanic. They must have heard what Morgan said—quiet was not Morgan's style—but neither of them appeared to take any offense.

Morgan jumped to her feet and cheered when Sean and his team skated onto the ice. She waved at him, but he didn't wave back. He was too busy fussing with his helmet.

"If you ask me, someone's trying to sabotage the game," Kevin Sloane muttered.

"What do you mean?" Morgan said, alarmed.

"Sean's helmet is missing. He looked everywhere for it."

"What's wrong with the one he has on now?" Morgan said.

"It's not his, that's what's wrong with it. You can see he doesn't like it. A guy needs his own gear. You hand someone a piece of replacement equipment right before a game and it can throw him off. Someone stole Sean's helmet. Someone's trying to sabotage the game by sabotaging Sean."

The players took their positions on the ice. The referee dropped the puck, and the game started. And you know what? It turns out that even if you're not a hockey enthusiast—and I'm not—it's still exciting to be sitting up close and personal in an arena packed with diehard fans who are screaming for their team in a play-off game. Even I could see how good Sean was. He seemed to be wherever the puck was a split second before it got there. Of course, that meant he was constantly dogged, blocked, and checked by the players on the opposing team. But by the end of the first period the score was 2–0 for Sean's team, and Sean had scored both goals.

When the period ended, he yanked off his helmet. He looked angry. Colin and Kevin both muttered under their breath.

Sean thrust the helmet at the referee. The ref handed it back. He and Sean got into an argument. Sean's coach intervened, and Sean said something to him. The coach spoke to yet another guy, who then made his way toward the locker room. The ref crossed his arms over his chest, waiting for something. He was looking directly at Sean. Sean scowled at the replacement helmet. He didn't want to put it back on, but the ref was insisting. Sean finally relented and went back out onto the ice.

Morgan whistled and waved to him. When Sean spotted her, his whole face changed. He smiled at her and blew her a kiss. As he did, I saw his eyes move around the arena, as if he were looking for someone else. I followed his gaze and spotted Tamara holding a microphone out to the coach of the other team. There was a cameraman nearby, focusing his lens on her. He seemed to be taking direction from a preppy-looking guy standing behind Tamara. But instead of paying attention to what the coach was saying into the microphone, Tamara was staring sullenly across the ice at Sean. He gave her a defiant look before skating back to join his teammates.

They listened in for whatever their coach was telling them. Player number 24, who was standing beside Sean, nudged Sean and said something to him. Sean said something back. Number 24 did not look pleased.

"What do you think that's about?" I asked Morgan.

"It looks like Sean and Jon disagree about something—again."

"Jon Czerny?"

Morgan nodded. "Sean calls him an enforcer."

"A what?"

"Muscle on ice. He keeps other players out of the way so that Sean can score. He gets into fights all the time. Guys have been injured because of him. Some players are afraid of him. I'm glad he's on Sean's team, because if he was on the other team, I'd be worried about Sean."

I saw what she meant during the second period. The opposing team scored one goal early on. Then Sean got control of the puck. He was skating for the opposing team's net when someone cut him off. Bang! Jon slammed that player into the boards. The guy collapsed on the ice.

"Good thing they wear all that gear," I said. "Shouldn't Sean tighten his chinstrap?" It was dangling in a loose loop from his helmet under his chin.

"They're supposed to wear them nice and tight. But a lot of guys in the NHL don't, so a lot of younger players think it's cool to wear them loose like that."

It looked like Jon wasn't finished with the guy who had collapsed. He raised an arm. He was going to hit the guy. Sean appeared and grabbed Jon's hand. Jon whirled around and shoved Sean—hard.

"Did you see that?" I said to Morgan.

"Sean says Jon plays too rough sometimes," Morgan said. "Sean doesn't like it, but he can't get Jon to stop."

Jon turned back to the player on the ice, but by then some of the guy's teammates had clustered around him and brought him to his feet. He looked shaken. As the ref checked the guy out, Sean was waved over to the side of the ice. His coach was holding something in his hands.

"It looks like they found Sean's helmet," Colin said. "Maybe now he won't be so distracted."

Sean took the helmet from the coach and jammed it onto his head. He fastened the chinstrap, but it hung loosely below his chin, just like it had on the other helmet.

Play resumed. A few seconds later, a player from the other team fell face-first onto the ice and a roar of disapproval filled the arena.

"What just happened?" I said, confused.

"Czerny tripped that guy," Colin said. "For no reason. What a dumb move. He's going to get a penalty."

Sean skated over to Jon. He looked angry. Then the ref signaled and, sure enough, Jon was sent off the ice.

When play got underway again, the game got rough. The players on the opposite team were one man up on Sean's team. I guess they didn't like what Jon had done. But he was sitting in the penalty box, so they took their anger out on Sean. They blocked him at every turn. Whenever he got control of the puck, three guys from the other team came at him to stop him from passing. The fans were going crazy. Morgan was sitting on the edge of her seat. I jumped up every time everyone else did, cheering Sean on and booing the other team.

Then it happened.

One of the players on the opposing team slammed into Sean. Sean shoved him. The other player pushed back and then dropped a glove and slammed his fist into Sean. Sean struck back. The other player grabbed at Sean's helmet. Then, I wasn't sure, maybe the other player pushed Sean or maybe Sean lost his balance. He flew backward toward the ice. I watched in horror as his unprotected head hit the ice.

Morgan leapt to her feet.

Every player on Sean's team sped over to where Sean was lying motionless.

Colin and Kevin Sloane rushed onto the ice.

Morgan pressed her hands against the Plexiglas that protected the spectators from wild pucks. Colin and Kevin knelt down next to Sean.

"He's not moving," Morgan said. Her voice was high and panicky.

"How did that happen? Why did his helmet come off like that?" I said.

"I don't know. It's not supposed to," Morgan said. "Robyn, he isn't moving."

Paramedics arrived. A hush fell over the arena.

One of the referees picked up the helmet and looked at it. Kevin stood up and took the helmet from the ref. Then he peered around the arena as if he were looking for someone.

I glanced at Morgan. She had tears in her eyes.

The paramedics were loading Sean onto a gurney. They wheeled him off the ice. For a moment it was completely silent in the arena, as if all the spectators were holding their breath. My eyes went to Jon Czerny in the penalty box. He hadn't moved. He just sat there, leaning forward, chewing gum with his mouth half open, as if he'd found the whole drama mildly amusing.

"I'm going to go and see how Sean is," Morgan said. She hurried away.

The referees cleared the ice. Someone made an announcement over the PA system: Sean Sloane, number 7, would not return to the ice tonight.

When the game resumed, the other team quickly scored another goal, which tied the game. Tension mounted in the arena. The other team kept attacking the net. Then Jon Czerny came out of the penalty box and everything changed again. He was all over the ice. He always seemed to be in the right place at the right time. His teammates kept passing to him the way they had passed to Sean. With ten seconds left to play, Jon scored the winning goal. The roar that went up was deafening. Jon pumped his arms as he glided around the rink.

As soon as the game was over, I went to look for Morgan. There was a knot of people outside the room adjacent to the team locker room. Most of them were reporters, including Tamara Sanders and her cameraman. The preppy-looking guy was there, too. They were all waiting to see how Sean was and, if possible, to get a comment from him. If Sean was in that room, I was pretty sure that Morgan would be there, too. So I waited with everyone else.

A few minutes later, the door opened and the reporters surged forward. A couple of cameras swung around, flooding the corridor with light. Sean emerged from the room with his coach on one side and Morgan on the other. His two brothers stood behind him.

Sean's face was pale. From where I'd been sitting, it looked like his head had hit the ice pretty hard. But he managed a shaky smile and told the reporters, "I'm fine. Really."

"What happened to your helmet, Sean?" someone called out.

"We'll be looking into that," Sean's coach said. "It's possible it was an equipment malfunction. But first we're going to get Sean to the hospital and have him checked over. I'll be issuing a statement about his condition first thing in the morning."

A dozen more questions were shouted out, but the coach held up his hands to signal that they would not be answered. He guided Sean through the crowd. Sean's brothers and the two paramedics followed closely behind him. I trailed after them, wondering what Morgan was going to do. I got my answer when they reached the ambulance. Sean kissed Morgan before getting inside.

"I'll call you," he said.

Sean's brothers got into a car and followed the ambulance out of the parking lot.

Morgan waited until the reporters had gone before she said, "They want to make sure that Sean didn't get a concussion."

"Talk about bad luck," I said. "First he had to play with a helmet he didn't like. Then his own helmet malfunctions. How can that even happen?"

Morgan's expression was grim. "The coach told the reporters that the helmet malfunctioned," she said. "But that's not what he thinks. He told Sean that it looks like someone tampered with it."

"Tampered with it?"

"With the strap that holds it on. It was cut almost all the way through. But whoever did it, did it really carefully, so that Sean wouldn't notice. Sean says the helmet was fine the last time he wore it. He always checks. But sometime between this morning and game time, his helmet went missing. He looked for it everywhere, but he couldn't find it. That's why he had to wear that other one for the first part of the game. But it wasn't comfortable, so he made them look for his helmet again. Now it looks like someone deliberately tampered with it."

"Who found the helmet?" I said.

"One of the assistant coaches. He went to the locker room to look one more time. He found it and brought it right out to Sean."

"And Sean didn't check it before putting it on," I said.

"It's his helmet. It was fine this morning. He assumed it was still fine. Besides, he was pumped for the game. He wanted to get back on the ice."

"So you think Kevin was right?" I said. "You think someone wanted to sabotage the game?"

Morgan shook her head. "I think someone wanted to hurt Sean."

"Who?" I said. "Why?"

She gave me a look that sent a chill through me and said, "You have to ask?"

"You can't mean Billy." But that was exactly what she meant. "Come on, Morgan. Isn't it more likely that someone from the other team did it? After all, it's the playoffs."

"League players aren't like that, Robyn. They may fight out on the ice, but they don't play dirty tricks—especially not dangerous ones like that."

"Maybe," I said. I didn't know much about hockey. I knew even less about hockey players. But I did know Billy. "You don't seriously think Billy would do something so dangerous . . ."

"Why not? He attacked Sean. He destroyed everything in his locker. He spied on us last night, Robyn."

So Sean had told her. "Billy hates Sean. And he knows all about hockey equipment—he played into middle school."

"But to deliberately hurt someone—"

"You're seeing only what you want to see," Morgan said. "You're not seeing what's really going on. Someone tampered with that helmet, and I'll bet you anything that it was Billy." She reached for the door.

"Where are you going?"

"To get my coat. I'm going to the hospital. I want to see how Sean is."

She didn't ask me to go with her, and I didn't offer. She disappeared inside for a moment and then strode to the bus stop. I started to shiver and zipped up my jacket. That's when I realized that my scarf was missing. I must have dropped it in the stands. I went back in through the team entrance and found the scarf under my seat. When I pushed open the door to go outside again, I heard angry voices coming from the parking lot.

". . . double-cross," someone said. "I should report you."

"And say what?" another voice said.

I held the door open just a crack so that I could hear what the voices were saying without anyone seeing me.

"You there!" A sharp voice behind me made me jump. "What do you think you're doing?"

I spun around and found myself face-to-face with the grizzled old man who had been guarding the team entrance before the game started. He was standing in a doorway to my left. I saw a battered desk behind him, along with a phone, an old computer, and a board on the wall that held dozens of keys. His office.

"You shouldn't be in here," he said gruffly. "I'm closing up."

"I forgot my scarf," I said. "I was just leaving."

I shoved the door open all the way and stepped out into the parking lot. It was deserted. Whoever had been out there was gone. I started for the street and . . . eeeew! I had stepped on something squishy. I lifted my foot. There was a huge, obviously fresh wad of gum stuck to the bottom of my shoe. Perfect.

.   .   .

I called Billy's house on my way home. No one answered. Billy didn't answer his cell phone either. I didn't talk to him again for a few days, and then it was under the worst possible circumstances.

CHAPTER **FOUR**

Sean didn't show up at school the next day, so right after the final bell, Morgan rushed over to his house to check on him. I went home. My mom called to say that she was working late and that I'd have to fix my own supper. After I'd eaten and put my dishes into the dishwasher, I called my dad. It was Thursday night. He and Nick were supposed to be doing something together. I'm not too proud to admit it: I was dying to know what it was.

He answered on the third ring.

"Robbie," he said. "What's up?"

I heard loud music in the background.

"Where are you, Dad?"

"I'm working. What can I do for you? Is everything okay?"

"Everything's fine, Dad." I tried to sound casual, even indifferent, as I asked, "Is Nick with you?"

"Robbie . . ."

"Come on, Dad. If you can't trust your own daughter, who can you trust?"

"I'm working," he said again, his voice firmer now. "I'd love to tell you all about it, Robbie, but I can't. Not now. Okay?"

It wasn't okay, but there was nothing I could do about it. I hung up without saying goodbye.

.   .   .

The next morning I got up, as usual, showered, as usual, dressed, as usual, and went downstairs to grab a bite to eat before heading to school, as usual. My mother was still home. She had the TV on so she could catch the morning news while she bustled around getting ready for work.

The phone rang. My mother answered it. She listened for a moment and then said, "She's right here." She handed the phone to me. "It's Morgan," she said. "I could be wrong, but it sounds like she's crying."

I sighed. One of two things must have happened: either Billy had done something stupid or Sean had dumped her. Whichever it was, I was in for an earful.

"Do you have the TV on, Robyn?" Morgan said. My mother wasn't wrong. She was crying. "Channel 2. Oh my god."

I reached for the remote, clicked to the right channel, and saw a reporter standing outside the hockey arena. There were police cars and yellow crime-scene tape in the background.

"What's going on, Morgan?" I said. "What happened?"

"It's Sean." She started to let out long, heart-wrenching sobs. "Oh, Robyn, he's dead. Someone killed him."

I stared at the TV again, but by then a different reporter was on the screen talking about a truck that had overturned on the expressway and backed up traffic for miles in every direction.

"Killed him?" I said. "What do you mean, killed him?"

My mom, who was at the front door with her briefcase in her hand, paused to look at me.

"Murdered him," Morgan said between sobs. "Someone murdered Sean."

My mom came back into the kitchen. "What's going on?"

"Morgan's boyfriend was murdered."

Her face went pale.

"Someone murdered Billy?"

"Not Billy. Sean Sloane."

Now my mom looked baffled.

"Long story," I said.

"Robyn, I'm at home. Can you come over?" Morgan said. "Please?"

"I'll be there as soon as I can."

My mother agreed to let me skip school for the day. "If that boy was as popular as you say, there isn't going to be much work done anyway. They'll probably bring in grief counselors." She checked her watch. "Grab your things, Robyn. I'll drop you at Morgan's house on my way to the office."

I reached for my backpack, which was already packed for a weekend at my dad's place.

.   .   .

Morgan's face was puffy, and she was holding a wad of damp tissues when she answered the door. She threw herself at me. I held her and asked her if she wanted me to make her a cup of tea. She trailed after me into the kitchen.

"What happened?" I asked while we waited for the kettle to boil.

She shook her head. "I don't know the whole story. I only know what I saw on TV. I couldn't believe it. I called Sean's house, but no one answered. Robyn, can you imagine how his parents and his brothers must feel?"

"I didn't see the news, Morgan. What did they say?"

"That he was at the arena last night, practicing."

"He was at the arena?" That didn't make any sense. "But he was injured."

"You don't know Sean," Morgan said. "He never lets anything come between him and hockey. The doctor said that he was going to have to miss a couple of games—playoff games—on account of what happened. But he told me he didn't want to lose his edge. He told me yesterday when I went over to his house that he was going to get some practice in. They said on the news that when his mother went to pick him up, she found him . . ." She started to cry again, and it was a few minutes before I could calm her down. I had just made tea when the doorbell rang. Morgan blotted her eyes with a tissue.

"Will you get that, Robyn? Please? I don't think I can face anyone."

The man in the dark overcoat standing on Morgan's front porch, waiting patiently for someone to answer the doorbell, was a homicide detective. His name was Charlie Hart. He was a friend of my father's.

"Robyn," he said, surprised. "I'm looking for Morgan Turner. Is she here?"

"She's inside. Come in."

He wiped his feet on the mat outside and again in the front hall and followed me through to the back of the house. Morgan was blowing her nose when I showed him into the kitchen. He introduced himself. He said that he was investigating Sean's death and that he understood from Sean's mother that Morgan and Sean were close. As soon as he said that, Morgan started to sniffle. Charlie Hart said he knew it would be difficult, but that he was trying to find out what had happened to Sean and that he needed to ask Morgan some questions.

"I'll be in the living room," I said.

Morgan grabbed my hand. "Stay with me."

I glanced at Charlie Hart, who nodded. I sat down beside Morgan.

"How well did you know Sean?" Charlie Hart asked Morgan.

"Pretty well, I guess." Her voice was small and trembling. "I was going out with him. We'd been seeing each other for a couple of weeks."

"When was the last time you saw him?"

"Yesterday. I went over to his house after school. He was injured playing hockey the other night and he missed school, so I went over to see how he was."

"Was anyone else there?"

"His mom was home for a while. But she had to go to work. His brother Colin came home just as I was leaving. I saw him sitting outside in his car. I knocked on the window and waved to him on my way down the driveway."

"Did you speak to him?"

"No. He seemed preoccupied. He was reading something."

"How were you and Sean getting along?"

"Fine."

"Did you and Sean have an argument or fight about anything last night?"

"No!" Morgan glowered at the detective.

"Do you remember what time you left Sean's house?"

Morgan glanced at me. I knew exactly what she was thinking: Why is he asking me all these questions?

"It was about six o'clock, I think," she said.

"Where were you between ten o'clock and midnight last night, Morgan?"

"I was right here."

"Was anyone here with you?"

"My parents. They were both here. I watched the eleven o'clock news with my dad. I didn't kill Sean." She was furious now.

Charlie Hart pressed on.

"Where are your parents now?"

"At work. Don't you believe me?"

"This is just routine. Can you tell me how I can get in touch with them?"

"I can give you their phone numbers."

Charlie Hart handed her a notebook and a pen. She wrote down her parents' work numbers. Then he said, "Did Sean tell you anything about his plans for last night?"

"Just that he was going to the arena. He wanted to practice."

"Did he say if anyone was going with him, or if he was planning to meet anyone there?"

Morgan shook her head. "I told him he should be careful that he didn't get hurt again, but he said no way. He said there wouldn't be anyone else there, so the only way he could get hurt was if he tripped over his own skates." A look of horror came over her face as she realized the terrible irony of what she had just said. I reached for another tissue and pressed it into her hand. "He—he said the arena wasn't even open last night, but that Wayne would let him in. Wayne is the janitor. He and Sean get along really well. Wayne lets him on the ice whenever he wants. He trusts Sean to lock up when he leaves."

"So as far as you know, Sean wasn't planning to meet anyone?"

"No."

Charlie Hart was quiet for a moment. A lot of people would have assumed that he was trying to think of his next question, but he wasn't. He knew exactly what he wanted to ask. He was just giving Morgan time to compose herself.

"Was Sean having trouble with anyone?" he said.

My whole body clenched up when I heard that question. I glanced at Morgan and willed her not to say anything about Billy. I was pretty sure that someone would eventually mention him if they hadn't already, but I didn't want it to be Morgan. Charlie Hart glanced at me. Then he turned his sharp eyes back to Morgan and waited for her to answer.

Morgan looked directly at the detective. "He was in a fight at school on Monday."

Charlie Hart's face was impossible to read, but I was willing to bet he already knew that.

"And ..." She hesitated and glanced at me. "Somebody vandalized his locker at school. And—" She stopped abruptly. "Maybe it would be better if Robyn wasn't here."

I tried to stay calm, but my cheeks burned. I stood up, walked out of the kitchen, and closed the door behind me.

It was twenty minutes before the door opened again. Charlie Hart nodded to me as he passed through the living room and then let himself out. A few more minutes passed before Morgan came out of the kitchen.

"He wants me to go to the police station and make a formal statement," she said.

"You told him about Billy, didn't you?"

"He would have found out anyway."

"But you told him. Morgan, you don't really think Billy had anything to do with what happened to Sean, do you?"

"I don't know what to think."

CHAPTER **FIVE**

I went from Morgan's house to my father's place. I was climbing up to my dad's third-floor loft when I heard footsteps coming down toward me.

It was Nick.

He looked as surprised to see me as I was to see him. Worse, he seemed uncomfortable at finding himself two steps above me in the stairwell. We stared at each other for a moment. Then, without a word, he brushed past me.

"Nick," I said.

He turned slowly.

"If you find it so unpleasant to be anywhere near me," I said, "maybe you should stop coming around."

His eyes were hard and distant. "I was just leaving something for your dad. I thought you'd be at school."

I turned away from him and continued on up the stairs. The whole time I was waiting for him to call me back and tell me that he was sorry and that he missed me.

But he didn't.

When I got up to the third floor, I saw a thick brown envelope leaning against my dad's door. Nick had said he'd left something. He must have meant that envelope. I picked it up, unlocked the door, and went inside. I tossed the envelope onto the dining room table, dropped my backpack onto the floor, and reached for the phone to call Billy. Still no answer.

.   .   .

My father got home just before seven. He was carrying two large paper bags.

"Chinese," he said, setting them onto the dining table. "Are you hungry?" He headed into the kitchen to get plates and cutlery.

"Nick left something for you," I said while I watched him set the table.

My dad glanced at the envelope but didn't pick it up. Instead, he started to open up containers of food— stir-fried vegetables, shrimp, beef in black bean sauce, steamed rice.

"Help yourself, Robbie," he said.

I sat opposite him and spooned some food onto my plate.

"What's going on with Nick, Dad? Why was he here? What's in the envelope?"

My dad heaped food onto his own plate.

"I missed lunch," he said. "You have no idea how

tempted I was to start eating while I was still in the car." He dug enthusiastically into the beef and black bean sauce.

"Nice try." I repeated my questions.

"Nick is a lot like your mother," he said. "He likes to keep his personal affairs private."

"Private from me, you mean," I said. "He seems to be getting along great with you."

My dad set his fork aside.

"I'm sorry things didn't work out between you and Nick," he said. "I don't think it was easy for Nick to come to me."

"Come to you for what?"

"He asked me not to say anything to you, Robbie. At first I agreed. But now . . . I told him yesterday that, under the circumstances, I was going to have to tell you something and that he had to make up his mind about what he was going to do."

"What do you mean?" I said. "Under what circumstances? What are you talking about, Dad?"

"You may run into Nick from time to time, Robbie. He's doing some work for me."

"What?"

"He's trying to get back on his feet."

After Nick had left town and had ended up in trouble—again—he'd come back to no job and no place to stay. He'd been living with his aunt on and off, but it never worked out. Nick didn't get along with his aunt's boyfriend. He didn't have parents to help him out. He had to support himself. My dad had let him have an apartment downstairs, but when Nick had got back to town, he'd decided not to move back in. Now that we were no longer together, he had even more reason to want to stay away. The last I'd heard, he'd been sleeping on a friend's couch.

"He called me two weeks ago and asked me if I knew of anyone who was hiring," my dad said.

"So you hired him?" I couldn't believe it.

"I gave him a few leads, but they didn't pan out. So I threw a little work his way."

"What kind of work?"

"Research. Gathering background information."

"Nick doesn't even have a computer."

"I gave him access to one. It turns out he's good at it, Robbie. He's tenacious, he's creative, and he's good at coaxing information out of people. He likes the work, too. But if it bothers you that much, I'll encourage him to look for something else."

Oh sure. Nick had finally found something that he was good at and that he liked. He was earning praise and being appreciated for it. And I could ruin it for him by whining to my father.

"Just because we're not going out anymore, that doesn't mean I don't want him to be happy," I said.

My dad picked up his fork again but didn't dig into his food.

"There's one other thing, Robbie," he said.

I waited.

"He needed a place to stay."

"Please don't tell me that you asked him to move in here, Dad."

My father shook his head. "But I gave him back his old apartment."

This was getting better and better.

"He's a good kid, Robbie. He needed a break, and I was in a position to give him one. That's all."

"It's okay, Dad," I said, even though it didn't feel okay.

I speared a piece of red pepper and put it in my mouth, but I couldn't tell you what it tasted like. All I could think about was that Nick was living right below where I was sitting. Every time I came in there was a chance that I'd bump into him on the stairs. There was a chance that I'd find him here in my dad's loft if I dropped by unexpectedly. I had been having enough trouble keeping my mind off him. I had broken up with Ben because I couldn't stop thinking of Nick, even though it was obvious that he wasn't interested in me. Now it was going to be hard to avoid him.

I decided to change the subject. "Dad, did you hear about that murder at the arena?"

"The hockey player?" I nodded. "I heard something on the news. Why?"

"Morgan was going out with him."

My dad looked surprised. "But I thought she and Billy—"

I filled him in on what I knew, which included how Billy had been acting. Then I asked the question that

I had been trying not to think about ever since I'd left Morgan's house.

"Dad, you don't think that Billy . . . that he would . . ."

My dad swallowed a piece of chicken.

"Do I think it's possible that Billy killed this kid?" he said. "Stranger things have happened, Robbie. When people get swept up in strong emotions, anything is possible." Nick was a case study in that. "But, seriously, do I think that Billy would kill another human being? No," he said firmly. "No, I do not."

I wished that Morgan could see things the way my father did.

·   ·   ·

I found my dad at the dining room table the next morning, a mug of coffee in one hand, the newspaper spread out in front of him. He turned when he heard me behind him. The somber expression on his face scared me.

"Sit down, Robbie," he said.

"Is something wrong?"

He nodded at a chair. I pulled it out and dropped down onto it.

"The police have made an arrest in the Sean Sloane murder," he said.

"Already? Did they find a witness or something?"

"They have a witness who says they saw someone at the scene of the murder. They also found the murder weapon in that person's possession. It had that person's fingerprints on it. He also has a motive, but no alibi. It sounds like it's a slam-dunk."

"So that's good, right?" I said.

My dad looked me directly in the eye. "The person they arrested—it's Billy."

CHAPTER SIX

"You're kidding," I said, even though I was sure this was something my dad would never kid about. I reached for the newspaper. There was an article in it about the murder and the arrest, but it didn't say much. It didn't even name the person who had been arrested. It just said that it was a male youth.

"How do you know it's Billy?" I said.

"Your mother called."

"Mom? What does she—"

"Billy's parents called her. They want her to represent Billy."

If Billy's parents had called my mom, then what my dad was saying was true. But my brain was saying, *No, no, no, it's not possible.*

"Billy didn't do it," I said.

My dad didn't say anything.

"He didn't do it, Dad."

"Robbie, we're just going to have to wait and see."

Last night he had seemed so certain that Billy could never take another life. Now he sounded as if he thought it might be possible after all.

My cell phone rang. It was Morgan.

"They arrested Billy," she said.

"I heard. It has to be a mistake. It just has to."

"I talked to Sean's brother Kevin," Morgan said. "It doesn't sound like a mistake. It sounds like he really did it. Do you know what that means, Robyn? It means that I spent the past five months going out with a murderer."

"He's not a murderer, Morgan."

I glanced at my father, who kept his eyes firmly on his newspaper.

"What's the matter with you, Robyn?" Morgan said. "Didn't you hear what I just said? Why are you always taking Billy's side?"

"Because he's not a killer, Morgan. You know he isn't."

That's when Morgan did something that she had never done before, no matter how angry she was.

"She hung up on me," I said to my dad.

He looked up from his newspaper. "This will probably be rough, Robbie. If I were you, I'd try to stay neutral."

"I've been trying to stay neutral. What else can you do when your best friend cheats on your other best friend? But you know what? It doesn't work because Morgan is completely unreasonable. One minute she's in love with Billy. The next minute she calls him a stalker and a killer. If you were me, and one of your friends had just been arrested for murder, the very last thing you'd do is stay neutral—and the first thing you'd do is try to figure out what really happened."

"Robbie," my dad said, his voice gentle now, "you told me yourself how Billy has been behaving. And you know the case against him—he had a grudge against the victim, he was found with the weapon, he was at the scene. Motive, method, opportunity. It's the trifecta of homicide."

I stared at him in disbelief. "What are you saying, Dad?"

"Sean was killed by a blow to the back of the head, which means that whoever did it hit him from behind. It wasn't a fight. It wasn't self-defense. Someone came up behind Sean and hit him hard enough to kill him." I didn't want to believe what he was telling me. "When Sean's mother found the body, Sean's face was covered. It was covered after Sean was dead. Murders don't usually cover their victims' faces after they kill them, Robbie—unless they feel remorse." He peered at me with his slate-grey eyes. "Does that sound like anyone you know?"

What was wrong with everyone? "It's a mistake. It has to be. Billy would never do anything like that."

My dad didn't say anything.

"Charlie Hart is working on the case," I said.

"I know. Your mother told me. He's a good cop, Robbie. Cautious, too."

In other words, Charlie Hart wouldn't have arrested Billy unless he was sure that he had a solid case. If there was some way the situation could have been worse for Billy, I couldn't think of it.

"When did you talk to Mom?"

"She called me this morning. She wanted me to give you a heads-up."

I punched in her cell-phone number. She answered on the third ring.

"Mom, I want to talk to Billy."

"He's in custody, Robyn."

"But he can have visitors, right?"

"He can see his lawyer and his parents. Robyn, I really think it would be better—"

"He's my friend, Mom. Don't you think he would want to know that someone besides his parents and his lawyer cares how he's doing?"

I heard my mom sigh at the other end of the line. "I'll see what I can do," she said. "I'll talk to his mother and see if she can get you approved. But it won't be today. Okay?"

"Thanks, Mom."

I got dressed and headed for the door.

"Where are you going?" my dad said.

"For a run. I have to think."

I made record time going down the stairs. I didn't want to take the chance that I'd bump into Nick. I ran all the way to the river that cuts through the city, and then I ran north along it, my feet pounding on the cement path as I thought about Billy. He couldn't possibly have killed Sean Sloane. He rescued injured birds. He fought to stop animal testing of cosmetics and pharmaceuticals. He volunteered at an animal shelter that had a no-euthanasia policy. He was the most humane person I knew.

On the other hand, he had gotten into a fight with Sean, which I wouldn't have believed if I hadn't seen it with my own eyes. He had phoned Morgan repeatedly, almost obsessively, even after she had asked him to stop. And he had been caught spying on her while she was with Sean. Lately, Billy had been doing a lot of things that were out of character. But still, murder?

I hated to admit it, but my dad was right, at least about one thing: when people get caught up in strong emotions, they do crazy things. I had seen that happen to Nick. I'd seen it happen to other people, too. And because of that, I could picture the events surrounding Sean's death.

I could picture Billy going to the arena. I could picture him seeing Sean there and maybe going over to talk to him, to tell him to stay away from Morgan. Sean had been killed by a blow to the head from behind—and now that I had seen Billy kick Sean in the schoolyard, now that I knew how much he was hurting, I could picture him picking up something and maybe lashing out at Sean. Not meaning to kill him, but maybe, because of what he was feeling, meaning to hurt him. I could picture Billy standing there and looking in horror at what he had done and then covering Sean's face in remorse before turning and fleeing from the scene. I hated myself for it, but I could picture it.

The rest of the day dragged by. I tried to do homework, but I couldn't concentrate. I picked up the phone a dozen times to call Morgan and put it down again just as many times. She had hung up on me. She should call back.

But she didn't.

I went out and rented a couple of DVDs and popped them into my dad's DVD player, but they washed by my eyes like boring scenery outside a speeding car. All I could think about was Billy.

On Sunday my dad said he had to drive out to the country to talk to some potential clients. He asked if I wanted to go with him. I said no.

"A change might do you good, Robbie," he said.

I told him I had to go to the library. I said I had an assignment due. I don't know if he believed me or not, but he kissed me on the cheek before he left and he said he'd try to be home for dinner. After he'd gone, I wrote him a note and left it on the dining table. Then I went to my mom's. At least she was doing something to help Billy. She was surprised to see me. When I asked her if she thought Billy had done it, she said, "That's up to the prosecution to prove. And it's up to me to make sure that he has the best possible defense."

"But he says he didn't do it, right, Mom?"

"Robyn, if there's a trial, you could be called as a witness. It's inappropriate for me to discuss this with you.

You know that." Then she said, "You can see Billy tomorrow after school."

. . .

I didn't see Morgan until French class, which was just before lunch. But then, I hadn't exactly been looking for her. I was still angry that she had hung up on me and never called back to apologize.

Morgan and I sit side-by-side in French. Usually we talk to each other before class. Sometimes we pass notes to each other during the lesson. But today I approached the classroom nervously, wondering what kind of mood she would be in and how she would treat me.

She didn't get to class until the late bell rang, and then she slipped into her seat without looking at me. I tried to catch her eye a couple of times, but she refused to turn in my direction. As soon as the end-of-class bell rang, she hurried to the door. It was the last straw. She was supposed to be my friend. Friends don't treat friends like poison. I ran after her.

"Morgan," I called.

She kept walking. I had to move fast to dart in front of her and block her way. I'd been planning to give her a piece of my mind, but when I got a good look at her, I felt a little less angry. Her face was pale, and there were dark circles under her red and puffy eyes. She hadn't bothered with makeup.

"How are you doing?" I said.

"My boyfriend was murdered. How do you think I'm doing?"

I wanted to say, *But he's only been your boyfriend for a few weeks.* I wanted to say, *Someone you've known your whole life has been arrested for murder.* Instead, I said, "I bet you haven't been eating right. Come on. Let's go to the cafeteria."

She stared at me. I was sure she was going to walk away, but she surprised me.

"Okay," she said in a whisper.

When we got to the cafeteria, she said, "Billy's mother called me."

I waited.

"She wants me to go and see Billy. She said it would mean a lot to him."

"And?" My fingers were crossed.

"I told her I couldn't. Robyn, it was one of the hardest things I've ever done, harder even than breaking up with Billy."

"You told her no?" I couldn't believe it.

"Of course I told her no." She seemed astonished by the question. "You're not going to see him, are you?"

"Yes, I am, Morgan, he's my friend."

"What about me? I thought I was your friend."

"You are. You and Billy are my best friends."

"You put me and Billy in the same category, after what he did?" She shook her head. "You have to choose. Either you're my friend or you're his. And if you're mine, you won't go and see him."

"Morgan, I have to. I—"

"Fine," she said. She turned and marched out of the cafeteria.

. . .

My mother picked me up after school and drove me to where Billy was being held. We had to sign in at the front desk and go through a security check. My mom walked with me to the visiting room.

"I'll wait out here," she said. "You go in. They'll bring Billy down."

I sat down to wait and was shocked when Billy finally appeared. He's tall and thin—really thin—even though he has a huge appetite. But now he seemed so fragile that a gentle breeze could have blown him over. His face was a greyish color and his blond hair was greasy and matted in the back, as if he hadn't bothered to wash or comb it in days. He sat down opposite me at one of the visiting tables.

"Are you okay, Billy?" I asked.

Instead of answering my question, he asked one of his own: "Have you seen Morgan?"

I nodded.

"I asked my mom to call her and ask her to come and see me. Did she say anything to you about that? Do you know when she's coming?"

"No, I don't."

Billy looked down at the tabletop. He took a couple of long, deep breaths before raising his head and fixing his pale blue eyes on mine.

"She doesn't think I did it, does she, Robyn?"

I felt terrible. How many lies was I going to have to tell him?

"She's pretty upset about what happened," I said. That was true. "But she's known you forever, Billy. She knows the kind of person you are." That was also true, even if Morgan wasn't exactly focusing on it right now.

"They arrested me, Robyn. They came to our house with a warrant. They searched the house and the yard. My mom was freaking out, and she doesn't do that very often." Billy's mother is a successful businesswoman. "My dad's working out of the country, so he couldn't help. Then they arrested me. They put handcuffs on me and took my rights, Robyn. The neighbors were all watching. Then they put me in a police car and they took me downtown.

"My mom phoned your mom, and she came down to the police station. She was with me while they asked me questions. That was the only time I wasn't one hundred percent scared, Robyn—when your mom was there. Then I was only about ninety percent scared. The cops think I did it. They think I killed Sean."

I looked into his blue eyes and saw a hundred different Billys: little Billy, from kindergarten, his hair so blond it was almost white, his hands covered in finger paint. Billy and Morgan and me out on the frozen lake up at Morgan's cottage one winter, skating from the island where the cottage was to the town on the opposite shore. Billy and Morgan and me in junior high, organizing a pet pageant to raise money for Billy's favorite animal-rights group. Billy and Morgan and me downtown so early in the morning that it was technically still night, rescuing injured birds that had crashed into office towers and taking them to Billy's rescue organization for treatment. Billy in the cafeteria at school, working up the nerve to ask Morgan out that first time.

"What did the police say?" I asked.

"That someone saw me go into the arena the night Sean was killed."

"Did you? Go into the arena, I mean?"

He hesitated before finally nodding. "I—I called his house. I wanted to talk to him. One of his brothers answered. He told me that Sean wasn't home, that he was at the arena, practicing." He shook his head. "I know I shouldn't have called, but I wanted to talk to him. I had to talk to him, Robyn. He didn't really care about Morgan. I know he didn't. But I do. I wanted him to leave her alone."

I sighed. He kept refusing to accept what had happened between Morgan and Sean. If anyone had told me a year ago that Billy would be so crazy about Morgan that he'd go off the deep end when their relationship ended, I would never have believed it. Up until recently, we were all just friends. Good friends. Best friends. I don't even think Billy noticed most of the time that Morgan and I were girls.

"So when you found out he was at the arena, you decided to go and talk to him in person?"

"I know what you're thinking," Billy said. "It was a stupid move, especially after what happened in the schoolyard."

That's exactly what I was thinking.

"At first I wasn't going to do anything," Billy said. "I kept telling myself I should let it go. But I couldn't stop thinking about Morgan. So around ten o'clock, I went to the arena."

"And someone saw you?"

"The head janitor. When I got there, he was just coming out. He smiled when he saw me, like he was expecting me. It turns out he thought I was Sean's ride. Apparently Sean was waiting for someone to pick him up. When I said I was looking for Sean, he told me where he was and asked me to remind him to lock up when he left. Then he went out to the parking lot. He must have sat there for a while, because his car was still there when I left."

"So he saw you come out again?"

"I guess," Billy said.

"You guess? The cops didn't say anything about it?"

"No. But if he was still there, he must have seen me. I remember wondering if he'd forgotten something. I wish he had. I wish he'd gone back inside after I left. Then he would have seen that Sean was still alive."

"What exactly happened when you went inside?"

"Sean saw me. He skated over to the boards and asked me what I was doing there."

"What did you tell him?"

"That I wanted Morgan back."

"Billy—"

"I know," he said. "You think I'm pathetic. Poor Billy—his girlfriend dumps him and he goes to the new guy and begs for her back. But it wasn't like that, Robyn. She didn't just dump me. He stole her. Sean stole Morgan from me."

"Billy, you can't steal a person."

"Yes you can."

What I meant was, *You can't steal a person who doesn't want to be stolen*, but I couldn't bring myself to say the words.

"I heard him, Robyn. I heard him say he was going to do it. And then he did it."

"What are you talking about, Billy?"

"I was out near the bleachers one day at lunchtime, waiting for Morgan. Sean was talking to his brother. He said if he wanted to, he could get any girl he wanted. He said he'd already picked one out. He pointed to the door, Robyn. And do you know who was coming out of school right then?"

"Morgan?"

Billy nodded. "You know what Sean said? 'Piece of cake.' Those were his exact words. And you know what else, Robyn? He saw me. Sean saw me. He knew I was going out with her. And he knew I'd heard what he'd just said. He smiled at me, like he was daring me to do something about it."

"You didn't say that to the cops, did you, Billy?"

He shook his head. "Your mother didn't let me say very much."

"Did you tell her what you just told me?"

He shook his head again. "We talked about some stuff. Mostly she asked me a bunch of questions. Do you think it's important? Do you think I should tell her?"

I didn't know what to say. But I hoped that if Billy ended up on trial, I wouldn't get called as a witness. I hoped no one would make me swear to tell the truth, the whole truth, and nothing but the truth—because then what would I do?

"What happened next, Billy—at the arena, I mean?"

"After I told Sean that I wanted Morgan back, he laughed at me. Even I could see that I wasn't going to get anywhere. So I left."

"That's it? You just left?"

He hung his head.

"Well," he said slowly, "I kind of shoved him first."

Terrific.

"I was leaving, and he came off the ice and started hassling me. So I shoved him. And he shoved me back, a lot harder. I fell into a pile of scaffolding—you know, from that work they're doing in there."

"Did you get into a fight with him after that, Billy?"

"No," he said without a second's hesitation. "I don't like the guy, but I'm not crazy, Robyn. He was in his hockey gear. He was wearing pads and a helmet and he had a hockey stick. You think I'd have a chance against that?"

It was the first sign of straight thinking I'd heard from Billy in a long time.

"So what did you do?"

"I left. I went home. The next day I heard he was dead. Then the cops came to the house with a search warrant. They said they knew I had been at the arena—"

"Because the janitor saw you."

He nodded. "They knew all about what happened at school, too. But, Robyn, the worst thing is, they found a piece of pipe. They said it was a piece of scaffolding from the arena. There was blood on it. They're testing it for Sean's DNA. There were fingerprints on it, too. It turned out they were mine."

I swallowed hard. It was as bad as my father had said—maybe even worse.

"Where did they find the pipe, Billy?"

"In my dad's shed."

"How did it get there?"

"You won't believe me if I tell you."

"Yes, I will. I promise."

He drew in a deep breath. "It was stupid. The morning after I went to the arena, I was out back getting the trashcans and the recycle bins, you know, to put them out for pick-up, and I saw this piece of pipe lying in the yard, like someone had dropped it. And, well, you know my dad."

When he wasn't out of the country working on mega-engineering projects, Billy's father loved to tinker. He had a backyard shed that Billy's family called his shop.

"I didn't know it was from the arena. It just looked like a piece of pipe to me. So I picked it up and put it in his shed."

That would explain Billy's fingerprints. But obviously the police hadn't bought his story.

"Dumb, huh?" Billy said. "If I'd put it in the garbage, it would have been picked up before the cops came to the house. Maybe then they wouldn't have arrested me. I didn't do it, Robyn. I didn't kill Sean. You believe me, don't you?"

His eyes burned into me while he waited for an answer.

I nodded. Firmly. "I believe you, Billy."

"What do you think is going to happen?"

"If you didn't do it—"

"It looks bad for me, Robyn. I'm scared."

"My mom's really good, Billy. Everyone says so."

"I know. But the thing is, it's not like the cops are looking for anyone else. They think I did it. They have a lot on me."

That was an understatement.

"Your mother couldn't get me out on bail. She tried, but she said with a murder charge, they usually keep you locked up until the trial date. You remember those guys that kicked that kid in the park, Robyn?" People who had kicked a child to death. "I heard they were locked up for a year and a half before their case even went to trial. A year and a half. I don't know if I can stand being locked up for that long. You don't know what it's like in

73

here. There are guys in here who are really messed-up. And they can really get to you, you know?"

I wanted to touch him. I wanted to hug him and re-assure him, to tell him it was going to be okay. But one of the rules was no touching. All I could do was look across the table at him and say, "You have to be strong, Billy."

"It's not easy," he said. "Especially in here, when people think you killed someone. There's a couple of guys, they keep asking me about it. And when I don't answer, they get mad." He let out a long, shuddery sigh. "Will you come back and see me again, Robyn?"

"Of course."

"Will you talk to Morgan? Will you tell her what I said?"

"I'll try, Billy."

I was glad he didn't ask me whether I thought she would listen, because I didn't want to have to lie to him again.

CHAPTER **SEVEN**

Sean's funeral was held on Tuesday morning. The church was jam-packed. All of Sean's friends and neighbors were there. And practically the whole school.

I saw Sean's brothers right up front. A man and woman were with them. I assumed they were Sean's parents. Morgan was with the family. From where I was, the middle of the church, I could see that she was crying. Colin put his arm around her to comfort her.

Sean's oldest brother, Kevin, delivered the eulogy. He talked about how Sean had driven the whole family crazy when he was a kid because he always had a hockey stick in his hand. If he wasn't playing on the ice, he was playing ball hockey in the street. His room was plastered with hockey posters. All Sean cared about was hockey, and his obsession had paid off. It wasn't long before he was out-scoring his brothers. Kevin said that it hadn't been easy to concede that his kid brother was a better player. But he said that they were all proud of Sean. They were proud that he had been scouted by big colleges, that he would have been offered a full scholarship wherever he went. Would have been. Morgan wiped her eyes.

Colin and Kevin and four of Sean's hockey teammates, including Jon Czerny, accompanied the casket down the aisle at the end of the service. Sean's parents followed them. His mother was leaning heavily on his father. Sean was going to be cremated, so there was no trip to the cemetery. I followed everyone to a reception in the church hall.

I'd been to a few funerals, and I always found it strange to see people eating and chatting, even laughing, afterward, while family members tried to put on a brave face. I saw some friends from school and drifted over to talk to them. I looked around for Morgan and spotted her standing next to Kevin. They were talking to Sean's hockey coach. I was trying to work up the courage to go and talk to her when a woman I didn't know came up to me and handed me a huge empty tray.

"Be a dear," she said. "Take this into the kitchen and bring out some more sandwiches."

To be honest, I was relieved to have something to do.

I passed Jon on the way to the kitchen. Now that the service was over, he had taken off his tie and undone the top two buttons of his shirt. He winked at me as I went by. I ignored him.

I pushed open the kitchen door and stepped right into the middle of a family scene.

"You should have been there," Sean's mother was saying, sobbing and angry all at the same time. She was talking to Colin. "You told me you were going to pick him up. He was waiting for you. If you'd been there like you said you would, it would never have happened. My baby would be alive."

"Laura," said Sean's father. "No one can say what might have happened. It's not fair to blame Colin."

"He's older," Sean's mother said. "Kevin and Colin know, they both know—the older ones look after the younger ones."

"But he—"

"It's okay, Dad," Colin said. He looked miserable.

Sean's mother started to cry in earnest. Sean's father—I later found out that he and Sean's mother were divorced—tried to put an arm around her to comfort her, but she pushed him away. That's when Colin spotted me.

"What are you doing here?" he demanded.

"Yeah," said a voice behind me. Morgan's voice. She had opened the door to the kitchen but hadn't closed it again. "You didn't even know Sean."

Being Morgan and being angry, she was also loud. I was sure that everyone in the hall could hear her.

"I'm here because I care," I said. "And because I know Sean was important to you."

"You went to see Billy." She made it sound like an accusation. "His mother called me again last night. She told me you went. She asked me to go, too."

"Billy asked me to ask you—"

"I told you, Robyn. I said you had to choose—and you chose Billy."

"He didn't do it," I said, keenly aware that no one who was watching me believed in Billy's innocence.

"They found the weapon in his dad's shed. It had his fingerprints on it. What part of this don't you get, Robyn?" She was screaming at me now. The room behind her went silent. "I think you should leave," she said. Colin went to her and slipped an arm around her.

"Morgan," he said. "Calm down. It's okay."

"I want her out of here." Morgan glared at me as tears ran down her cheeks. "I want her out of here."

I turned and fled from the hall.

.   .   .

I should have gone back to school, but what for? I knew I wouldn't be able to concentrate. So instead I started walking. The tears that I had managed to hold in when I left the church hall started to dribble down my cheeks. I kept seeing Morgan's angry face. She hated me. She didn't want me anywhere near her. Morgan and I had been friends for as long as I could remember. We had always gone to school together, always hung out together, always trusted each other. Until now. Now I was the enemy, and all because I knew what she should have known—that the sweetest, kindest guy in the world would never commit murder. What was the matter with her?

I hadn't had a destination in mind when I'd left the church, but I guess my feet had their own idea because I ended up on my dad's street, looking up at his loft. I stood there for a few moments before deciding that the day had been bad enough. The last thing I wanted to do was run into Nick. I turned to leave—and there he was, coming toward me, his dog Orion's chain leash in one hand, a book in the other. I might have slipped by him unnoticed—he was reading while he walked—if Orion hadn't barked and lunged at me.

"Whoa, boy," Nick said, holding the leash tightly and looking up. His eyes met mine. At first they were cold and hard, but they softened a little as he studied my face. "What's wrong?"

"Nothing."

"You've been crying. I know you, Robyn. You don't cry over nothing. Is it about Billy? Your dad told me what happened."

"Morgan thinks he did it."

"And you don't." It was a statement, not a question. "Did you talk to him?"

I nodded.

"He's scared, Nick. They're keeping him in custody until the trial."

"It can be hard in there," Nick said. "Most people they lock up, if they're not messed up when they put them in there, they get messed up pretty fast afterward. If you see Billy again, tell him the best thing is to keep to himself and not to talk to a lot of people about his life or the case. And tell him that if anyone gives him any trouble, he shouldn't just take it. If you don't stand up to the bullies in there, they just make it harder. It's better to fight back, even if you end up getting hurt. If you cause the other guy some pain, he'll think twice about coming at you again."

And there I was, fighting tears again. Nick could take care of himself. He'd learned how—the hard way. But Billy? Billy wasn't a coward, but despite what had happened outside school, he wasn't a fighter, either. Billy believed that if you treated people right, they would treat you right.

"Crying won't help, Robyn," Nick said.

He was standing close to me now, and I wished more than anything that he would hold me. But he didn't.

"You helped me a couple of times," he said. "You stood up for me when nobody else believed me and nobody else cared. You can help Billy, too."

"This is different, Nick. This is murder."

He stared into my eyes.

"I know what he feels like, Robyn. He needs to know that there's someone on his side, someone who believes him, no matter how bad it looks. He needs it more than anything, especially if some people think he did it."

Nick was right. The fact that Morgan was convinced of Billy's guilt made it all the more important that I stand by him—whether Morgan hated me for it or not.

"Thanks," I said.

"Hey, Robyn? If there's anything I can do . . ."

But there wasn't.

He tugged gently on Orion's leash and headed for the door to my father's building. I opened my mouth. I came close to calling him back and telling him that I wasn't with Ben anymore, that I wanted to be with him instead, that I wanted us to be together again. But in the end, what was the point? If he was interested in being with me, he would have said something by now. Maybe he wouldn't have come right out and told me, but he would have given me some clue.

I turned and walked away, and as I walked I thought about Sean Sloane. There were only two ways to look at his death: either Billy had killed him or he hadn't. If he hadn't, then someone else had. The question was, who?

CHAPTER **EIGHT**

Later that night I was sitting in the room in my mother's house that my father used to call his den but that my mother calls the family room. I was half-studying and half-watching TV, something that I could get away with only because my mom had stayed late at the office again. But my mind kept drifting to Billy and how scared he had looked the last time I'd seen him. I also thought about what Nick had said—how tough it could be, being locked up, and what some of the kids were like.

I thought about something else Nick had said—that Billy needed someone to believe in him, no matter how bad things looked. It was obvious Morgan wasn't going to be that person, so that left me. I decided that I was going to believe Billy, even if, in some deep corner of my mind, I could see how maybe he could have done it—not intentionally, but in the heat of the moment. I was going to believe him because he was my friend, because he's one of the most decent people I know, and because I wanted to think that if I ever found myself in a similar situation, someone would believe me.

Okay then.

Billy hadn't done it.

So who had?

I picked up the TV remote and started surfing through channels, *click, click, click,* rhythmically, while I pondered the question.

Sean's face flashed before my eyes for a second and then was gone.

I blinked. Was I seeing things?

I clicked back couple of channels and there he was again—Sean Sloane, on TV, looking handsome and very much alive. It was some old postgame footage. Sean had been good-looking in real life, but he was movie-star gorgeous on the TV screen. No wonder Morgan had fallen for him. His interviewer was an equally attractive young woman—Tamara Sanders, Sean's ex-girlfriend.

Tamara had been at the arena the night of Sean's accident. I had heard her talking to him outside the players' entrance. It sounded as if she were begging him to do something that was important to her—probably the documentary that Morgan had said Tamara wanted to do on Sean—but he had told her no. Just how important was that project to Tamara? Important enough that his refusal had made her want to get even? I made up my mind to find out.

.   .   .

Going to school the next day was torture. I spotted Morgan at the end of the hall while I was on my way to my first class. She looked directly at me before turning and disappearing around the corner. When I got to French class, she had traded places with someone else and was sitting up front. When Madame Leclos asked Morgan why she had moved, she said she was having trouble seeing the chalkboard.

Right.

Morgan was also in my math class. There, she sat two rows behind me on the opposite side of the room. But if she got to class before me, she usually waved at me on my way in. Not today. She didn't even look in my direction. As soon as the bell rang, she scurried out of class and disappeared in the crowded hall.

Fine.

At lunchtime I made my way to the cafeteria and stood near the door, scanning faces, searching for Tamara.

I didn't see her. But I did spot a girl named Lissa who I had seen hanging around with Tamara. She was sitting with Colin Sloane. It wasn't until I was halfway to their table that I saw who was sitting next to Colin—Morgan. Colin had slung his arm casually over the back of her chair. I hesitated and was about to retreat when Morgan's eyes met mine. The expression on her face made me feel about as welcome as wasps at a picnic. How could she be like this?

I steeled myself and made my way to their table.

"Hi, Morgan," I said. I don't know why I bothered.

She looked away as if she hadn't heard me.

I turned to Lissa.

"I was wondering if you've seen Tamara around," I said.

Colin leaned over and whispered something in Lissa's ear. She frowned at me.

"So what if I have?" she said.

"I'm looking for her."

Colin looked at me with undisguised hostility. "You're friends with the kid who murdered my brother."

I could have argued with him—about the murder part, not the friend part—but it would have got me nowhere. Instead, I concentrated on Lissa.

"Do you have any idea where Tamara might be?" I said.

"My mother found Sean," Colin said. "Did you know that?" He had a loud, booming voice, but it quavered when he spoke to me. "How do you think she felt when she saw him lying there?"

Morgan laid a hand on his arm. "It wasn't your fault, Colin," she said gently.

"I should have been on time," Colin said. "If I'd got there when I was supposed to, Sean would be alive." His voice broke. I couldn't help feeling sorry for him. His mother had made it clear that she blamed him for what had happened.

Morgan squeezed his arm and held it for a moment. Lissa gave me a dismissive look. No one said another word. I had no choice. I turned away.

Someone touched my sleeve as I made my way toward the cafeteria door. It was Dennis Hanson, math wizard and champion bird-rescuer.

"Tamara's at the TV station," he said. His head was slightly bowed, and he didn't look directly at me. "She spends most of her lunches there. She's working on a program."

"Thanks, Dennis," I said.

"But you can't just walk in there," he said. "Not without an appointment. If you want me to, I could get you in."

"You can?"

"My dad works there. I heard someone say you're helping Billy."

"That's right."

"I can get you in," he said again. He still didn't look at me.

.   .   .

The local public broadcasting station where Tamara hosted a show for teens was two blocks from school. Dennis and I walked there together. I tried a couple of times to make conversation but got nowhere. I thought maybe he was shy, but when we got to the TV station he wasn't at all intimidated by the high-security reception area with security cameras and electronic-pass entry system. He marched right up to the receptionist and, without looking directly at her either, said, "My friend wants to see the station."

The receptionist greeted him with a smile, gave us two security passes, and let us through.

"Be careful on the third floor, Dennis," she said. "They've been painting every night since last week. There's wet paint everywhere."

Dennis led the way to the elevator.

"Tamara is probably in Editing," he said. "I'll show you where it is."

We rode up to the third floor. When the elevator doors opened, I was overwhelmed with the smell of fresh paint. There were ladders, drop cloths, and paint cans everywhere.

Dennis told me how to get where I was going.

"I'll wait for you here," he said.

I followed his directions to a door marked Editing. There was a schedule tacked to a small bulletin board on the wall beside the door. Sure enough, Tamara's name was printed neatly in one of the boxes. I peeked through the window. The room appeared to be newly painted. Corkboards and framed pictures leaned against a couple of filing cabinets, waiting to be remounted. Tamara was working at a computer at the back of the room. The same preppy-looking young man who had accompanied her and her cameraman to the hockey game was bent over her. I pushed open the door.

The man straightened up quickly when he heard the door click back shut. There was a pink glow to his cheeks. Then Tamara looked up. Her cheeks turned red.

"What do you want?" she said.

"Can I talk to you for a minute?"

Tamara glanced at the preppy-looking guy.

"Yes, well, good work," he said. He nodded curtly and left the room.

Tamara watched him go before she turned her eyes on me.

"Do I know you?" she said.

Morgan was right about one thing: Tamara thought she was special—so special that she didn't recognize someone she had passed in the hall at school probably a couple of hundred times. I knew who she was, but she didn't know me.

"I was watching TV last night," I said. "I saw an interview you did with Sean Sloane. It was really good."

She leaned back in her chair and regarded me with new interest. "Another Seanette, huh?" she said.

"Excuse me?"

"Another little girl who had the hots for Sean."

"No. No, I—"

"Hey, I don't mean it as a put down. He was a good-looking guy. Fantastic athlete. Great body. Lots of fun—well, most of the time."

"Everyone says he was going to end up in the big leagues," I said. "In your documentary, you called him the next Wayne Gretzky."

"Yeah, except that from what I hear, Gretzky was always a gentleman. Always."

"And Sean wasn't?"

She laughed. It came out sounding bitter.

"But you went out with him, didn't you?"

"For two years." She studied me again. "No offense," she said. "But what do you want? Did you know Sean? Because I don't remember ever seeing him with you. And, believe me, I would have noticed."

"I'm a friend of Billy Royal."

Tamara's face changed the way the weather does when a storm front moves in.

"That's the kid they arrested for murdering Sean," she said.

I nodded.

"And you're friends with him?"

"He didn't do it."

"Yeah, right." She turned back to what she had been doing.

"That interview I saw last night was really good," I said again. "Sean was so hot. How come you didn't do a longer show on him? That could have really turned into something if he ever got drafted to the majors. You know, Sean Sloane, the early years."

"Don't think I didn't try," Tamara said. "His team was going to win the finals. And whether he took one or not, he'd been offered full scholarships. A lot of schools here were interested in him."

"What do you mean, whether he took one or not? I heard he was smart. Didn't he want to go to college?"

"That's what his mom wanted." Morgan had told me the same thing. "She really wanted him to accept a scholarship. It was a big deal for her. She wanted him to get the best education. I thought he wanted that, too. I mean, it's why he wasn't playing major junior. If you do that, you lose your NCAA eligibility. You can always go to school later, but Mrs. Sloane knew how that usually went. Most guys in major junior let their grades slide. They all think they're going to the NHL. Sean was really going to do it, though." She shook her head. "There was definitely an audience for a doc on him—all those hockey fans who love to spot the next Great One, all those kids who want to be the next Great One, and all the girls who want to be with the next Great One. He was going to beat the odds. He really was."

"What odds?" I asked.

"The one-in-a-million odds." When I still looked puzzled, she rolled her eyes. "Do you have any idea how many guys play minor hockey?"

I shook my head.

"Thousands," she said. "Tens of thousands. Maybe more. And they all dream of making it to the NHL. But the reality is that one in a thousand will ever get drafted—and a third of them won't ever play an NHL game. Only two in ten thousand will actually last a few years and have a shot at the big money. Everyone dreams, but hardly anyone makes it. Sean was going to make it, and everyone knew it. The thought of having to play NCAA for four years was really getting to him. It drove him crazy that his mom wouldn't let him play major junior like his brothers did. I talked a producer here into letting me do a special feature on him. I had a budget for it, everything. Sean agreed to it. Then, when we broke up—"

"I heard he dumped you."

Her cheeks turned red. "When he replaced me with that new little chicklette of his," she said, "he also backed out of the project. Do you have any idea how that made me look? I pitched my bosses on the piece. I promised them that I could deliver the goods. I told them he'd agreed to being interviewed and to having a camera on him during the lead-up to the playoffs. Then, at the last minute, he tells me to forget it." She shook her head in disgust.

"That must have made you angry," I said.

"You have no idea. I was ready to ki—" She looked at me. "Yeah, I was pretty mad."

Charlie Hart had asked Morgan where she was between ten and midnight the night Sean was killed. That had to mean that the police had narrowed the time of death to those two hours.

"Tamara, where were you the night Sean was killed?" I said.

She laughed. "What are you? A junior cop? I was here until midnight. I was editing a tape for an upcoming show. I had to give it to my producer the next day. You want to check with him?"

"Everyone liked Sean," I said. "Everyone said he didn't have an enemy in the world."

"Well, he had at least two," she said.

I waited.

"Your friend Billy, who killed him," she said. "And Jon."

"Jon Czerny? But he and Sean are—were—on the same team."

"Are you for real?" Tamara said. "Just because two guys are on the same team, that doesn't mean they're best buddies. Especially if they were both up for team captain and the one who got beat out is a bad loser. And if the one who got beat out had been pretty much guaranteed the position until the other one started making moves. At least, that's what I heard."

"Are you saying—"

"I'm not saying anything. Look, the cops have the guy who did it. I hear your friend is a lovesick puppy. But just for the record, Sean wasn't the angel everyone thought he was. He may have played like Gretzky on the ice, but he definitely didn't act like him off it." She turned back to her work, dismissing me once and for all.

I went back to where I had left Dennis. He hadn't moved a muscle. He was so engrossed in reading something on a clipboard that was sitting on a stack of paint cans that he didn't even look up when I approached him.

"Are you coming back to school, Dennis?" I asked.

It took a moment before he pulled his eyes away from whatever he was reading. I glanced at it—a schedule of some kind.

"Thanks for your help," I said as we rode back down to the main floor.

"I hope they let Billy go," he said. "Spring migration is going to start soon. The birds need him."

.   .   .

I admit it: after seeing how aggressive Jon Czerny could be on the ice, I was a little afraid of him. But according to Tamara, he had a strong reason to dislike Sean. And I remembered how he had shoved Sean during the game. It wasn't hard to picture someone who was that physical grabbing something and hitting Sean over the head with it.

I looked for Jon in the cafeteria. He wasn't there. I looked outside. He wasn't there, either. Then the bell rang and I had to go to class. As soon as classes were over, I did the rounds of the school—no Jon. Then I thought, *He's a hockey player, the championship is coming up, and his team has just lost its captain and star player. If I were Jon, what would I be doing now?*

I headed for the arena.

Sean's team was on the ice. At first no one noticed me. Then the coach skated over and waved me to the boards.

"This is a closed practice," he said.

"I just wanted to talk to Jon," I said.

The coach looked at me as if I were simple-minded. "He's not available right now."

"When is practice over?"

"We'll be another hour at least. If you want to wait for him, you'll have to wait outside."

As I left, I saw the coach skate over to Jon and gesture in my direction. Jon turned to look at me, but I couldn't read his expression from that distance.

It was chilly out in the early spring afternoon. The sun was already sinking toward the horizon. An hour later I was still huddled outside the players' entrance and was starting to worry that the team had gone out the main door instead. But there were still cars in the parking lot, and I hadn't seen anyone inside except the hockey team. I stomped my feet to stay warm and waited some more.

Eventually the door burst open and hockey players poured out. They were loud and boisterous, jostling and teasing each other. Jon was the loudest of the bunch, but he broke away from the pack when he saw me and loped over to where I was standing. His eyes ran over me, and he smiled.

"You were at the funeral," he said, chewing and snapping a wad of gum. "Sean's girl, what's her name—"

"Morgan," I said. Morgan would have been livid if she had heard herself referred to as What's-her-name.

"Whatever," Jon said. "She was screaming at you." He seemed to enjoy the memory. "Coach said you wanted to talk to me. What's up? You want an autograph?"

"Actually," I said, "it's about Sean."

The slick smile slipped from his lips. "Yeah. Too bad about what happened, huh? The guy was loaded with potential."

"I heard he was big-league material."

Guys were getting into cars and driving away. The coach was standing a few meters behind Jon, watching us.

"Czerny," he called. "You want a lift or what?"

Jon looked me over again. "There's a place across the street. Can I buy you a coffee or something?"

The way he was leering at me gave me the creeps, but I put Billy first and said, "Sure."

Jon turned to the coach. "Change of plans," he said.

"But we need to talk," the coach said.

"Later." Jon's tone made it clear that he considered himself to be in charge.

The coach stood there a moment before shaking his head, wheeling around, and heading for one of the few cars still left in the parking lot.

Jon and I crossed the street to a brightly lit diner and took a booth near the window. When a waitress appeared, Jon ordered a burger with fries and a chocolate milkshake.

"Practice," he said. "It takes a lot out of you, especially when it's playoff season."

The waitress turned to me.

"Hot chocolate, please," I said.

"So, you're a hockey fan, huh . . ." Jon began. He looked vaguely at me, and I realized that he had forgotten my name.

"Robyn," I said. "To tell you the truth, I don't know much about hockey, other than that everyone said Sean was going to be the next Gretzky."

Jon snorted. When I gave him a look, he shrugged unapologetically.

"Hey, I know you're not supposed to speak ill of the dead," he said. "But you know what? There isn't a hockey arena in the world that's big enough to hold Sean Sloane."

"I don't understand."

"His ego. It was huge. Yeah, he came across as Mr. Nice Guy. Sucked up to all his teachers. Sucked up to the coaches. Sucked up to those college scouts who were here. Mr. Suck-Up—that's what they should have called him. Or Mr. Manipulation. Hockey wasn't the only game he knew how to play."

"Are you saying he didn't deserve all the attention he was getting?"

The waitress arrived with my hot chocolate and Jon's food. Jon reached for the ketchup and drowned his burger in it. Then he poured ketchup all over his fries. I tried not to look at his plate when he dug in.

"I tell you what he didn't deserve," Jon said, his mouth full of burger and fries. "He didn't deserve to be team captain."

"But I thought—"

"At the end of last season, Coach told me he was going to make me captain. I care about my career, sure. But I also care about the team. A hockey team isn't just about one guy getting to shine. It's about the whole team battling its way to the playoffs and then getting a shot to prove that it's the best—not just one player. Sean—okay, so for a while he was a team player. But then he got the word that the scouts had an eye on him. A couple of them came up here, watched him, talked to him. They look at hockey skills first. But they also look at academics and character, that kind of stuff. Coach decided Sean would be a shoo-in if he was team captain. You know, if he showed real leadership skills. The next thing you know, I'm bumped."

"What do you mean, bumped?"

Jon shoveled a gigantic handful of fries into his mouth. "Coach calls me in and tells me, 'Hey, Jon, I know I promised you, but here's the deal with Sean.' You get it? Because the coach is ready to do anything it takes to make sure Sean gets his shot. Sean, not me."

"Did schools scout you, too?"

Jon stopped chewing. He glowered across the table at me, and right then I understood why, as Morgan had said, some guys were afraid of him.

"I got some interest," he said. "But with my grades . . . hell, who cares what my grades are like? I want to be a hockey player, not a brain surgeon."

"I guess some of those schools care—"

I shut up when he glowered at me again.

"Yeah, well, if Sean was such a great guy, how come that kid offed him? And I bet he wasn't the only person who wished Sean Sloane would drop dead. Look, I'm sorry for his parents. I'm sorry it happened. But you know what? It makes me sick how everyone is acting like the guy was a saint. He wasn't. Not even close."

"Now that he's gone, does that mean the team has no captain?"

He took a hearty sip of his milkshake. "I'm captain now. And it's my job to help the guys believe, really believe, that we can win without Sean. And you know what? We can. Sean was just one guy."

"But he was the best." When Jon scowled at me again, I hastily added, "At least, that's what everyone says."

"Yeah, well, everyone is just going to have to wait and see."

I thanked him for the hot chocolate.

"You got a boyfriend?" he said, looking me over again as I stood up.

"Yes." It seemed easier to lie than to have to fend him off.

He shrugged and turned his attention back to his food.

"Can I ask you something, Jon?"

He looked up from his plate.

"The night Sean died, he was at the arena alone, practicing. How come the rest of the team wasn't there?"

"It wasn't a practice night."

"Then why was Sean there?"

"His head hit the ice pretty hard when he had that accident. He was going to have to sit out a few games— you know, before he could get medical clearance. I guess he was afraid he'd lose his edge. Maybe he was also afraid the scouts would lose interest in him if they saw how well the team did without him."

"What was the rest of the team doing that night?"

"How would I know?"

"What were you doing?"

"What's it to you?"

"I was just wondering."

"Because of your friend, huh?" He shoved more fries into his mouth before answering. "I went downtown to pick up some protein-shake mix. Then I just walked around. You want to know what I was thinking about? I was wondering where I was going to be next year at this time."

"What do you mean?"

"I graduate this year. I don't want to go to college. I want to play hockey. I'm still hoping to make it to the major juniors, but who knows? For sure I have a shot. And it's the best way to make it, you know?"

I didn't.

"But, hey, after that last game, we're looking good for the championship. If we make it, that could be good for me. And now that Sean's not around to hog the lime-light, maybe I have a shot at getting drafted."

"Drafted?"

"You really don't know much about hockey, do you?"

I admitted that I didn't. After he explained the hockey draft to me, I said, "But what does Sean's death have to do with your chances of getting drafted? You said Sean was planning to go to college. He was going to play NCAA. He promised his mother."

Jon laughed. "You don't know hockey, and you don't know Sean. I said Sean could go to the college of his choice—if he wanted to. But all this season he was boasting that he could get his mother to do anything he wanted. She never let up about getting a good education, especially after the way his brothers turned out. But it wasn't just college scouts who were interested in him. The major junior scouts came around, too. And the NHL. He started to hear rumors about the draft and how he'd be a first-round pick for sure. How he'd get a great contract, make some serious money. Trust me, he was going to go for it."

"What about his mother?"

Jon shrugged. "All I know is what he was telling the team, which is that if he finished high school with a minimum B-plus average, he could sell her on anything."

"Since when do you need a B-plus average to be a professional hockey player?"

"He was going to tell her he was keeping his options open, that he could always go to college later if things didn't work out. He said she'd go for that. He said the important thing for her was that he didn't end up like his old man."

I remembered Sean's father from the funeral. He didn't look so bad to me.

"What about his dad?" I said.

"He was a hockey player too. I think he had maybe one season in the NHL, something like that. Sean said his parents got divorced after his dad was dropped from the roster. Last I heard he was a mechanic out west somewhere. Sean's mother wanted better than that for

Sean. He was her big dream, the one who was going to make it." He shook his head again. "Guess that didn't work out, huh?"

CHAPTER **NINE**

I told myself I wasn't going to call Morgan, but unless I wanted things to be over between us, one of us had to make the first move. *Maybe I should be the good guy*, I thought.

When she didn't answer and I heard her perky voice—"Hi, this is Morgan. Leave a message."—I got angry. I remembered what she had said to me after the funeral and how she had treated me at school. I thought about her refusal to visit Billy. Okay, so she wasn't going out with him anymore, but she had known him forever. If she'd been arrested for murder—even if it turned out that she'd actually *done* it— Billy wouldn't have hesitated even for a second to go and see her. Maybe Morgan really had loved Sean, although I didn't see how you could truly love someone you've only known a few weeks. That was no excuse for treating her friends the way she had. Besides, she was wrong about Billy. I ended the call without leaving a message.

Billy's mom called. She said that Billy wanted something from school—a picture that was hanging on the inside of his locker door. She asked me if I would get it for her. I knew the picture she meant. Poor Billy. Despite everything that had happened, he still hadn't gotten over it. He was still picking at the scab and making it impossible to heal. Having that picture in there with him wasn't going to make it any easier. But it seemed like the least I could do. I told his mother I'd get it and bring it over to her the next day after school. Then I tried to do my homework. Tried, but didn't succeed. My mind kept going back to Sean. What had happened to him at the arena that night? More to the point, *who* had happened to him?

.   .   .

Billy's locker was exactly nine lockers away from Morgan's. I had a pretty good idea how Morgan would react if she saw me getting that picture out of it, so rather than chance a run-in, I went to school extra early the next morning.

The hallways were deserted. Well, almost deserted. When I got to the second floor I saw someone opening a locker halfway down one of the halls.

Wait a minute.

The locker had a great big star on it. It was Sean's locker.

"Hey," I called.

The kid who had just opened Sean's locker spun around. It was Aaron Arthurs.

"What are you doing? That's not your locker," I said.

Aaron looked up and down the hall. He was probably checking to make sure that there was no one else around. When he saw the coast was clear, he said, "It's not yours, either, so back off."

I'd seen a lot of people give Aaron a hard time over the years. Usually he just turned red in the face, looked embarrassed or intimidated, and said nothing. But usually there were a lot of people around, watching and laughing. Now there was only me, and Aaron didn't seem remotely intimidated. Instead, he was surly and hostile.

"Maybe I'll buzz down to the office and tell Mr. Dormer that I caught you stealing from Sean's locker," I said. "Or maybe I'll find Colin and tell him."

The surly expression on Aaron's face vanished instantly.

"I'm not stealing. I'm taking back some stuff that Sean borrowed from me."

I couldn't imagine Sean even acknowledging Aaron's existence, much less borrowing anything from him.

"I'm going to the office," I said.

"Hey, wait a minute." He sounded panicky. "How do you think I got the combination to this lock?" That was a good question. "Sean must have given it to me, right?"

"It's a brand-new lock," I said. The vandal—named Billy, if you believed Morgan—had removed the original lock with a bolt-cutter two days before Sean was murdered. "Maybe he hadn't memorized the combination yet. Maybe you saw where he'd written it down. Or, wait. All locker combos are recorded in the school office! You're in the office a lot. Do you know where the combinations are kept? Did your mom tell you?"

Aaron's face turned scarlet. He reached up to the top shelf of the locker, pulled out a history textbook, and handed it to me.

"Look inside the front cover," he said. "Go on."

I opened it. The name printed inside was Aaron Arthurs, not Sean Sloane.

"He borrowed it from me after he lost his own," Aaron said. "He never got around to returning it. And, if it's okay with you, I don't want to have to pay for a new one if I don't have to."

I handed the book back to him. He stuffed it into his backpack, reached into the locker again, and removed two more books, leaving only a stack of binders, all looking neat and new, on the shelf.

"You want to look at these, too?" he said, holding the two books out to me.

I shook my head.

"I'm sorry," I said. I watched him close and lock the locker. "I didn't know you and Sean were friends."

He didn't answer. He just jammed the books into his backpack and walked away.

I continued down the hall and turned the corner to Billy's locker. I was reaching for the framed photograph that hung inside when someone behind me said, "What do you think you're doing?"

Morgan. What was she doing at school this early?

She stared stonily at me, then reached past me and snatched the photo from the hook Billy had attached inside the locker door. It was a picture of her and Billy, their arms around each other, both smiling contentedly at the camera.

"What were you planning to do with this?" she said.

"Billy's mother asked me to get it for B—"

She flipped the frame over, removed the back, yanked out the photograph, and thrust the frame at me. She tore the picture in half, then in quarters. She kept tearing until the pieces were as small as confetti. They fluttered from her fingers to the floor.

"Morgan—"

She turned and walked away.

. . .

The picture that Morgan had torn up was one that I had taken on New Year's Day. I had given a copy to Billy and another to Morgan. Billy had framed his and hung it in his locker. Morgan had stuck hers to the mirror in her bedroom where she could look at it as many times a day as she looked at herself. I was willing to bet that her copy was long gone.

I had also kept a copy for myself. I went home after school to get it and then slipped it into Billy's frame.

When I got to Billy's house, his mother was coming out the front door. She had her car keys in her hand and a worried expression on her face.

"I brought Billy's picture," I said.

His mother stared at it for a moment and shook her head.

"I know it's what he wants," she said. "But I'm almost afraid to give it to him. You know what I mean, Robyn?"

I knew exactly what she meant. Looking at that picture was like looking into the past—and the past is always gone for good.

As she got into the car, I said, "Would it be okay if I went with you to see him?"

She smiled gratefully at me. "I would really appreciate that, Robyn. And I know Billy would, too."

.   .   .

Billy's mother had to give the photo to him as it was, just the picture, no frame, no glass. Her lower lip trembled a little, but she nodded and said, "Of course."

Billy looked even thinner and paler than he had the last time I'd visited him. But he told his mom that he was fine, really—he was just having a little trouble sleeping. Still, she fussed over him for a few minutes before filling him in on the news from home. Billy's sister was expecting a baby and was busy decorating the baby's room. She had picked out names, too—Samantha if it was a girl, and Samuel if it was a boy. Billy nodded vaguely, but

I could tell he wasn't really listening. Finally his mom said, "Why don't I let you and Robyn have some time alone to catch up?" Before she left, she gave him the photograph.

Billy gazed at it. A little smile appeared on his lips. Then he turned the picture over and his smile vanished.

"This isn't the one that was in my locker," he said.

"It's the same picture, Billy."

"But it isn't mine. Mine has lipstick on the back. That's how Morgan autographed it for me. She kissed it."

"I'm sorry," I said. "I didn't know. I—I forgot to go to your locker, Billy. So I brought my copy instead."

He studied me for a few moments. "So you'll bring mine the next time you come, right?"

"Billy—"

He looked me straight in the eye, and I knew that he knew.

"Something happened to it," he said.

"I'm sorry, Billy."

"Did someone take it?"

I nodded.

"Who?"

"What difference does it make?"

"What difference does it make? They arrested me, Robyn. They think I murdered Sean Sloane. You think it doesn't make a difference to me that there are people who would go into my locker and take my stuff while I'm stuck in here? You think it doesn't make a difference to me who believes me and who doesn't?" He was talking so loud that the guard who was standing at the door turned to look at him. "I try not to. I try to get my homework done. I try to read. I try to keep caring about the stuff I've always cared about. But I can't help it. I think about who believes me and who doesn't. And I think about what it's going to be like if I get out of here and have to face all those people who think I killed someone. I think about whether they're really going to believe I didn't do it or whether they're going to think I got away with something. But you know what I think about the most? I think about what will happen if I get convicted, even though I had nothing to do with it. It happens, right, Robyn? The cops make mistakes. Innocent people end up in jail. Their lives get ruined."

"I believe you, Billy."

"That cop was here yesterday. He wanted to ask me more questions about what happened that night. He said it would go a lot easier on me if I cooperated. How can I cooperate when I didn't do it?"

"Billy, did you trash Sean's locker?"

His face hardened.

"Come on, Billy, I know you didn't kill Sean."

"Then why are you asking me about his locker?"

"Because someone killed him. People don't go around killing people for no reason. Someone must have had it in for him. If you didn't trash his locker, then someone else did—someone who had a grudge against him. Maybe a big enough grudge to want him dead." I hated to have to ask again, but I needed to know for sure. "So, did you do it, Billy? Did you trash Sean's locker?"

"No." His voice was defiant. He seemed to be waiting for me to challenge him.

"Okay," I said. "What about all the phone calls Sean was getting? Was that you?"

That earned me another indignant look.

"No."

"Morgan says you called her night and day."

"I wanted to talk to her."

"But you didn't call Sean?"

"I called him once—the night I went to the arena."

"Morgan said he was getting threatening phone calls."

"Not from me," Billy said. "I only called Morgan."

"What about the day before Sean was killed? Did you go to the arena on Wednesday, Billy? Maybe after I saw you outside school, after Sean threatened you?"

"The police asked me the same question. And the answer is no. I was nowhere near the arena that day."

"Did they believe you?"

"They had to. I have an alibi for the whole day."

I waited, but he didn't tell me.

"Where were you, Billy?" I said finally.

His eyes slipped away from mine.

"What's the matter, Billy?"

He looked doggedly down at the tabletop.

"Billy?"

"I was with Ben."

"Ben? I didn't know you and Ben hung out together."

Billy knew Ben, of course. So did Morgan. And I knew they both liked him. But it had never occurred to me that either of them would spend time with him now that Ben and I had broken up.

"We don't exactly hang out together," Billy said. "But I wanted to talk to him, you know, because he—well, just because."

"Because why?"

Billy shifted his gaze back to the tabletop.

"Billy?"

"Because I thought he would understand how I felt."

He meant because I had broken up with Ben like Morgan had broken up with him. And for more or less the same reason—because of another guy.

"I'm sorry, Robyn. I wasn't going to say anything, but . . ."

"It's okay. You can spend time with anyone you want. You don't need my permission."

"I called him, and he said he had Wednesday off school to volunteer." Ben goes to a private school that is very big on community service. "He invited me to go with him. I met up with him after I saw you at school . . ."

"After you tried to see Morgan again," I said gently.

He nodded. "He picked me up just up the street, like we arranged. We spent the day at an animal shelter in the west end. They just finished adding a new wing, and they had a whole bunch of volunteers there painting, getting the place ready for the animals. There were lots of people who saw me there all day, Robyn. Afterwards I went over to Ben's house. I was there until eleven at night. I told the police that. They took his name and everything. They must have checked with him. I had nothing to do with what happened to Sean at the hockey game."

Well, that was something.

"Maybe whoever sabotaged Sean's helmet decided to go even further," I said. I wondered if Charlie Hart had thought about that. But why would he? He had an eye-witness who placed Billy at the scene of the crime just before Sean's body was found. He had found the murder weapon on Billy's property, with Billy's fingerprints on it. What difference would it make who had tampered with Sean's helmet when all the evidence pointed to Billy? Billy even had a history of attacking Sean. I looked across the table at Billy and realized that he'd never told me the whole story about that.

"What happened the day you got into that fight with Sean? Why did you go after him like that?"

Billy hung his head again. "He said something. He said something and I . . . I just lost it." He looked up at me. "I know how that sounds. If I could lose it like that and attack him, I could also kill him, right?"

"I didn't say that, Billy."

"But I didn't kill him."

"What did Sean say that made you so mad?"

Billy let out a long shuddery sigh before leaning across the table. In a soft voice, he repeated what Sean had said. Then he sat back in his chair and looked at the floor.

"You know what, Billy?" I said. "If he had said that to me, I think I would have jumped him, too."

Billy's head bobbed up. He almost smiled.

The guard who had been standing at the door came over to where we were sitting.

"I have to go," Billy said. "Thanks for coming, Robyn. And thanks for the picture."

"No problem," I said.

Billy had stood up, preparing to leave, when I called to him.

"Hey, Billy? How is Ben, anyway?"

"He misses you," Billy said. "He asked me if you were seeing Nick, but then he said never mind—he didn't want to know. Other than that, he's okay, I guess." He turned, walked to the door, and waited for the guard to open it for him. Only after he was gone did I realize that I hadn't asked him how he was doing in there. Or whether he was still scared.

CHAPTER **TEN**

Billy had said that he hadn't made threatening calls to Sean. He'd said he hadn't trashed Sean's locker. He had an ironclad alibi for the day of Sean's accident—there was no way he could have tampered with Sean's hockey helmet. So who had done all those things? And how big a grudge did that person have against Sean? Big enough to want him dead?

Try sleeping when you have questions like that scurrying around in your head like squirrels in an attic.

I reached for my phone and made a call.

"Sure," my dad said after he listened to my question. "I've been stumped plenty of times before."

"What do you do when that happens, Dad?"

"What's this about, Robbie?"

"You have to ask?"

There was silence on the end of the line.

"Dad?"

I thought maybe he'd lecture me about letting the police do their job. But he didn't.

"So the question is, what do you do if you have a gut feeling that something is true, but no hard evidence to back you up? Is that it?"

"Something like that."

"You chip away at it. You work with what you've got, even if it's not much. And you have faith that it will lead you somewhere else. It's the only thing you can do."

"That's it?"

"Pretty much. Detective work isn't linear, Robbie. No straight line guaranteed to get you from point A to point B. There could be a million possible ways, and you have to figure out for yourself which one makes the most sense."

"Thanks, Dad."

I was about to hang up when he said, "Ask me what I was doing on Thursday night."

"What you and Nick were doing?"

"Yeah. Go ahead. Ask me."

"I thought it was top secret."

"It was. It isn't anymore. Come on. Ask me."

I knew he was trying to make up for not telling me earlier, but now that I knew that Nick was working for him, I didn't really care what they had been doing. The less I knew, the better. But a peace offering is a peace offering.

"Okay, what were you doing on Thursday night, Dad?"

"Hal was in town."

Hal is an old friend of my father's. They went to high school together. Hal manages an old rock band.

"To do a music video," my father added.

"With the dinosaur band?"

"Hey, those guys aren't much older than me," my father protested.

"Exactly," I said.

"Hal is also managing a new group," my father said. When he told me which one it was, I couldn't help being impressed.

"They were here?"

"One night only, to shoot their new video. Took them all night to shoot it. They'd work for three hours on something that will take up maybe fifteen seconds in the final video."

"I can't believe they were here and you didn't tell me."

"I wanted to, but work is work, Robbie, and this really was top secret. Even the press didn't get wind of it."

"It couldn't have been all that top secret. You told Nick."

"Nick was working with me."

"On security? Isn't he a little young for that?"

"Not for that part of the job. All he had to do was help make sure no one got near the site who didn't belong there. Hal gave me an autographed poster for you. I'll give it to you the next time you're over."

"Thanks, Dad. And thank Hal for me the next time you're talking to him."

By the time I got out of bed the next morning I had a plan. Okay, it wasn't much of a plan, but as my father had said, you have to start somewhere.

I had two places to start: Tamara Sanders and Jon Czerny. Sean had promised to cooperate on a documentary that could have boosted Tamara's budding TV career. Then he had dumped both her and his promise. As for Jon Czerny—not only was he jealous of Sean, Sean had stolen the team captainship from him. Now that Sean was gone, Jon was back on top. Had he killed Sean to get what he wanted?

All I had were questions and suspicions. But that was better than nothing. I figured Tamara's alibi would be easy to check. She had said that she was in the editing room at the TV station the night Sean was killed. So that's where I decided to start.

As soon as I got to school, I went looking for Dennis Hanson. I finally spotted him in a crowded hall at lunchtime. I elbowed my way toward him and grabbed his arm to get his attention. He let out a shout, as if I had bitten him, and frantically jerked free of me. Every head in the hall turned to see what had happened.

"Sorry. I didn't mean to startle you," I said. I wished people would stop staring at us—at him. "I need your help. I'm trying to help Billy, but to do that I need to go back to the TV station. I have to find out who was in the editing room the night Sean was killed."

"Painters," Dennis said.

"What?"

"Painters were in Editing."

"How do you know that?"

"I saw the schedule when we were at the station. Painters were in Editing on Thursday, 8 P.M. to 2 A.M."

"Are you sure?"

He nodded but didn't look directly at me.

"Dennis," I said, "is there any way you could find out if there was anyone in the room while the painters were there?"

"I could ask my dad."

"Would you? It's for Billy."

"Okay," he said. "We can go now."

. . .

Dennis's father had a large office on the top floor of the public-television building. The sign on the door said "VP, Programming." I assumed Dennis would knock before entering. I was wrong. He just opened the door and walked in and didn't seem to notice the surprised looks on the faces of the three men sitting around a conference table. The youngest of the three was the same preppy-looking guy I had seen with Tamara.

"Dennis," said one of the other men, "I'm in the middle of something here." He didn't seem at all perturbed by Dennis's sudden appearance, so I assumed he must be Dennis's father. "Ed," he said to the older of the two men with him. "You remember my son Dennis." Then he turned to the preppy-looking guy. "David, I don't believe you two have met. This is Dennis. Dennis, this is David Roberts. He produces the teen show."

David stood up and thrust out a hand, which, of course, Dennis didn't take. He didn't make eye contact with David either. David awkwardly withdrew his hand.

"Aren't you going to introduce your friend, Dennis?" Mr. Hanson said.

"Her name is Robyn," Dennis said.

"I go the same school as Dennis," I said. "And I'm sorry to disturb you. We can wait—"

"The painters were in Editing last Thursday night, right, Dad?" Dennis said. "They were there for six hours, right? That's what it said on the schedule. Editing, 8 P.M. to 2 A.M. Right, Dad?"

Mr. Hanson looked surprised by the question. All he said was, "Well, I'm not sure."

"Robyn needs to know. It's important, right, Robyn?"

"Well, I—" It was obvious we were interrupting a meeting. "It can wait, Mr. Hanson. I'm sorry we disturbed—"

"But you said it was important," Dennis said. "She needs to know, Dad."

Mr. Hanson looked quizzically at me but didn't press the point. "If it's that important, Dennis, I can certainly check. If you and Robyn wouldn't mind waiting—"

"I saw it on the schedule," Dennis said. "She needs to know right now."

"Well—" I glanced around the room. Ed's face was impassive. But he had met Dennis before, perhaps under similar circumstances. David didn't look as unruffled as Ed. He shifted uncomfortably in his chair.

"If you'll excuse me for a moment," Mr. Hanson said. He went to his desk, picked up the phone, punched in a few numbers, and asked someone if the painters had been in Editing last Thursday.

"Ask him what time they were there," Dennis said, "and who was in the room while they were working."

I glanced at Ed and David again. Ed was studying some papers on the table in front of him. David's eyes darted nervously from Dennis to Mr. Hanson.

"Thank you, Louis," Mr. Hanson said. He hung up the phone. "You were right, Dennis," he said. "The painters were there from 8 P.M. to 2 A.M., just as you said. They were there alone. Everything in the room was covered up to protect it from the paint. That's why they're doing all the painting at night—to minimize the disruption around here. Now, is there anything else I can do for you, son?"

"No," Dennis said.

"I'm really sorry we interrupted you, Mr. Hanson," I said.

"No problem," he said graciously. He walked us to the door and showed us out.

.   .   .

I found Tamara at her locker after school.

"I was at the TV station at lunchtime," I said.

"So I heard." Her acid tone made me think that my suspicions were right.

"You lied to me, Tamara. You said you were working in the editing room when Sean was killed. But you weren't. The room was being painted that night. The only people in it were the painters."

She grabbed me by the arm, dragged me into the nearest empty classroom, and shut the door.

"I don't know what you think you're doing," she hissed.

"Did the police talk to you after Sean was killed?"

She stared angrily at me but didn't answer.

"Of course they did," I said. "They talked to everyone who knew him. Did you tell them the same thing you told me—that you were in Editing between ten and midnight?"

Her face flushed. "What difference does it make where I was? I didn't kill Sean. Your friend Billy did. He was practically stalking Sean because of What's-her-name."

"Billy says he didn't do it, and I believe him."

"Well, good luck to him," Tamara said.

"You and Sean weren't exactly on the best terms. You told me yourself that he bailed out on that documentary. Did you tell the police about that, too?" The alarm in her eyes told me she hadn't. "I bet Sean bailing on you didn't do much for your reputation at the station. How did your producer take the bad news?"

"David knows it wasn't my fault."

"I heard you at the arena the night Sean was injured. You were begging him to reconsider, but he wouldn't. He wouldn't even listen to you. Sure, he was going out with Morgan. But you can go out with someone else and still be friendly with your ex-girlfriend. Sean didn't want to have anything to do with you, though. Why is that, Tamara? Why was he so mad at you? What did you do?"

"Who says I did anything?"

"The cop who's investigating Sean's death—he's a friend of my dad's," I said. "I know him pretty well. And I'm sure he'd be interested if I told him that Sean's ex-girlfriend had a very good reason to be angry with Sean and that she'd lied about where she was at the time he was murdered. I bet he'd want to have another talk with you, Tamara. I bet he'd want to know where you really were."

Her face turned white.

"I didn't have anything to do with what happened to Sean."

"Where were you?"

She looked down at the floor.

"Fine," I said. I started past her.

She grabbed my arm again. "If I tell you, you have to promise you won't tell anyone."

"First you tell me where you were. Then I decide who I tell or don't tell."

She seemed to be struggling with what to do. "I was with David."

"David Roberts? Your producer?"

122

She nodded. So I'd been right. I remembered the way Sean had scowled at him at the hockey game. I remembered how flustered David had been when I caught him bent over Tamara the first time I had talked to her and how uncomfortable he had been when Dennis and I had turned up in Mr. Hanson's office. I was positive that it was David who had told Tamara that I had visited the station again today.

"Are you and he—"

She nodded.

"We've been seeing each other for a couple of months. But if anyone at the station finds out, he could get into trouble. It doesn't look good for a host to be dating her producer. People could get the wrong idea."

A couple of months?

"But I thought you and Sean didn't break up until a couple of weeks ago," I said.

"We didn't," she said. "I'm not even sure how it all happened. David and I were working together. Then we started seeing each other outside of work. He and I have a lot in common—a lot more than Sean and I did. And he's only a couple of years older than me. But . . ." She hesitated again. "I didn't want to tell Sean. I was afraid if I did, he'd back out of the documentary. And I wanted that story. You have no idea how much it could have helped my career."

"What happened? Did Sean find out?"

She nodded. "He came to the station when I wasn't expecting him—sweet-talked his way past the receptionist. Sean could sweet-talk his way past anyone. He was a real charmer."

It seemed like everyone said the same thing about Sean—and they all said it with the same bitterness and disdain.

"He caught David and me together," she continued. "He was furious. He told me that was it, no documentary. He said we were through. I tried to apologize, but . . ." She shook her head. "You don't know what he could be like. I had him on my show five times. I talked one of the sports guys at the station into doing a feature interview with him. Okay, so I should have broken up with him before I started seeing David. But I got Sean a lot of publicity. And you know what he said to me? He said he'd never do another interview with me again, ever. And he said he'd tell the station exactly why he'd backed out. He was also going to put it out there that I only got my job because I was seeing David—and that's not true."

Sean sure knew how to get even with someone. But I didn't feel too sorry for Tamara either.

"Do you think he really would have told the TV station about you and David?"

"You didn't know Sean," she said. "He could be really vindictive. And mean. He told me he could replace me in a second. He even told me who he was going to replace me with."

I listened in stunned silence while she told me the whole story.

"You're kidding," I said when she had finished. "I thought he was supposed to be a nice guy."

"Yeah, he was a real prince," Tamara said sourly. "But I didn't kill him. If they have to, the police can ask David where I was. But I wish they wouldn't. I really like my job, and I worked hard to build a good reputation. Are you going to tell them?"

"Not if I don't have to, I guess. But I want you to do something for me in return."

I could see the apprehension in her face.

"I want you to talk to someone for me," I said.

CHAPTER ELEVEN

A car pulled up in front of the restaurant where Tamara and I were waiting. Morgan got out. She said something to the driver—it took a moment before I realized that it was Colin Sloane—and the car drove away. I ducked out of sight until Morgan had entered the restaurant, found Tamara, and settled opposite her in the booth. Then I slid onto the bench beside her, blocking her exit.

"What do you think you're doing?" she said, scowling at me.

"You've been avoiding me."

"Maybe that's because I don't want to talk to you. And if you don't mind, I'm here because she asked to see to me." She nodded at Tamara.

Tamara looked pointedly at me. It didn't take long for Morgan to get the message.

"I should have known something was up when she called me out of the blue like that," she said.

"I asked her to," I said.

Morgan was already pushing against me, trying to force her way out of the booth.

"There's something you need to know, Morgan," I said. She refused to look at me.

"Sean didn't dump me so that he could go out with you," Tamara told her. "He dumped me because he found out I was cheating on him. He started going out with you to get back at me—and at your boyfriend."

Morgan turned furious eyes on Tamara. "I don't believe you."

Tamara looked evenly at her. "Were you in any of Sean's classes?"

"No."

"Were you one of his hockey groupies?"

"Of course not!"

"Did you even go to his hockey games?"

"No."

"Did you talk to him much before you started going out with him?"

"Not exactly."

"Did you talk to him at all?"

"Well, no."

"So what happened?" Tamara said. "Did he just come up to you one day and ask you out?"

"Something like that," Morgan said. "I was helping set up a display in the hall, and I noticed Sean watching me. We started talking, and the next day he asked me out."

"Just like that?"

"Yes."

"And this was when?" Tamara said.

"About a month ago."

"Sean found out about me and David exactly one month ago," Tamara said. "He didn't waste any time."

"I still don't believe you," Morgan said.

"Believe me or not, but it's true," Tamara said. "Sean was angry at me for cheating on him. He asked you out to get back at me—and because he saw a chance to get even with your friend Billy."

"Billy? Why would Sean want to get even with Billy?"

"Sean didn't like him."

"Sean didn't even know him," Morgan said.

"Sure he did. From a long time ago. And he had a grudge."

"Billy never said anything to me about Sean," Morgan said. "If there was some kind of grudge between them, he would have told me."

"Are you sure about that?" I said. "When was the last time Billy ever held a grudge—against anyone? But Sean . . ."

Morgan's eyes flashed with anger. "You put her up to this, Robyn."

"No, she didn't," Tamara said. "And I'm telling you the truth." She dug in her purse and pulled out a sheet of paper, which she unfolded on the table in front of her. A photocopy of a newspaper clipping. "I did a little research before I came here." She pushed the clipping across the table to Morgan, who stared at it suspiciously. When she had finished reading it, she slid the clipping over to me.

Five years ago, Billy and Sean had faced each other at a peewee hockey game. Sean had been twelve at the time and Billy eleven. Each was the highest scorer on his team. According to the article, an altercation broke out at the game. One person was quoted as saying that Sean was too aggressive as a player and that he "attacked" one of Billy's teammates. Someone else was quoted as saying, "Aggressive play is what hockey is all about." Whether it was an attack or just hockey, Billy went to his teammate's rescue. When he pulled Sean off the other player, Sean tripped—at least, that's what it had looked like to the reporter—and took a bad fall. He had to sit out the rest of the season.

"Billy never mentioned that," Morgan said.

"Sure he did," I said. "He said some kid got hurt at a game and it was his fault. He felt terrible about it. He moped around for weeks. Then he stopped playing league hockey."

"That's why he quit?" This seemed to be news to Morgan, even though she and Billy and I had been close in those days. But Morgan had always been more interested in herself than in anyone else, and, until recently, she had never been tolerant of boy pursuits like hockey.

"Sean never forgot," Tamara said. "He had to sit out the championships that year. And he and his brothers were super competitive. All they cared about was hockey. If Sean's mom didn't have a rule that he had to keep up his grades to stay in the game, he would probably have spent all his time on the ice instead of just most of it."

Morgan shifted beside me.

"Sean's brother Kevin barely scraped through school," Tamara said. "And he had so many injuries on the ice that he can't play anymore. The closest he can get to hockey now is being assistant coach for a junior team. His other brother, Colin, had three serious concussions. He's waiting for clearance to get back on the ice. If he does, he might have a shot—a long shot—at being drafted. But he's no scholar either. He'll be lucky to graduate high school. Sean was the star of the family. He was supposed to get a good education and be the next Gretzky."

"Except I heard he wasn't going to college after all," I said.

Tamara's eyes widened in surprise.

"Who told you that?" she said.

"You didn't know?"

"No."

"You remember you said the thought of waiting four years before going pro was really getting to Sean?"

She nodded.

"Well, Jon told me that he'd been boasting to the team that he was going to play major junior. He thought he might even get drafted. If he did—and Jon seemed to think he would—he was going to tell his mom that he would continue his education later. That's why he was keeping his grades up. He thought that if he could convince his mom that he could get into college whenever he wanted to, she wouldn't mind if he put hockey first for a while."

"I don't know about that," Tamara said. "Maybe he could have talked her into it. He sure knew how to manipulate people. But she wouldn't have been happy about it. Sean could be a real jerk, but he cared about his mom. He really did. If you want my opinion, it would have broken her heart."

Morgan was still staring at the newspaper clipping. "Are you seriously telling me that Sean went out with me so that he could get even with Billy for something that happened five years ago?"

"Sean pointed Billy out to me a bunch of times," Tamara said. "He told me what happened. He made fun of him all the time—he's an animal lover, he's a vegan, he quit hockey because he couldn't handle it. Sean even shoved him around a couple of times—I saw him do it."

"Billy never said anything to me," Morgan said.

"You know Billy," I said. "It takes a lot to get him riled up."

"I heard someone say that Billy saw you and Sean together at Sean's house," Tamara said. "I bet you anything Sean knew he was there. I bet you he put on a real show for him."

Morgan's face turned pink. I had the feeling that Tamara was right.

Tamara looked across the table at me. "So," she said, "are we good? Or are you going to tell on me?"

"If I have to say anything, I'll let you know first," I said. "I promise."

She eyed me closely, as if trying to decide if she could trust me. Finally, she nodded. Tamara got up and left. I slid out of the booth and took a seat opposite Morgan. She stared at the newspaper clipping for a few moments before looking at me.

"Do you think she's telling the truth?" she said.

"I don't know why she'd lie."

"Maybe she killed Sean."

"She has a pretty good alibi, Morgan."

"And Billy doesn't. If everything she said is true, it gives Billy an even stronger motive to kill Sean."

I shook my head. "Think about it. Billy quit hockey because he felt responsible for Sean getting hurt. Billy's never intentionally hurt anyone in his life. Yeah, he was at the arena that night. He went there to talk to Sean because he heard Sean boasting about how he was going to score with you. He knew Sean was just using you, and he wanted to ask him to stop. Billy wanted you back, Morgan. And he swears Sean was alive when he left."

"You really believe him, don't you?" she said. This time she didn't sound angry.

"Of course I do. I know Billy. And so do you. Besides, he has a solid alibi for the hockey helmet incident. He was with Ben. They were at an animal shelter together. Dozens of people saw them. They were there all day."

"What about Sean's locker? Billy was at school that day when he shouldn't have been."

"He snuck in to leave that letter in your locker."

"He could have trashed Sean's locker while he was there. He could have made all those calls to Sean too. And he did attack him. I saw the whole thing."

"Did you?" I said. "The whole thing?"

"What do you mean?"

"Tell me exactly what you saw."

She frowned. "Well, Sean and I came out of the school. We were going to get something to eat across the street. We were hurrying because we wanted to make sure we got a booth. Then someone called to Sean. A friend of his—Matt. Sean went back to talk to him for a minute. I didn't pay any attention until I heard Matt tell Sean to look out. That's when I turned around and saw Billy. He looked so angry, like he was ready to ki— he looked like he hated Sean. And the next thing I knew he'd jumped him. I'd never seen Billy do anything like that before."

"Did you hear anything?"

"Like what?"

"Like what Sean and Matt were talking about?"

"No. Why? What am I supposed to have heard?"

"You weren't supposed to hear anything," I said. "But according to Billy, Sean said something—about you. And Billy got angry."

"What did he say?"

"Why don't you ask Matt?"

"Why don't you just tell me what Billy said?"

"Trust me. Ask Matt. Please, Morgan?" I wanted her to hear what had really happened from someone besides Billy and me. I wanted her to believe it.

"Okay," she said. She sounded uncertain for the first time in a long time. "But what about that pipe the police said was the murder weapon? Billy's fingerprints were on it."

I told her what Billy had told me.

"Someone could have thrown it into Billy's yard," I said. "It was public knowledge that Billy and Sean had been in a fight at school. All Billy did was pick it up and put it in his dad's shed."

"According to Billy."

"According to Billy." I stood up. "Talk to Matt. See what he says. Then call me."

I left her sitting in the restaurant, staring at the newspaper clipping.

. . .

I know it sounds crazy, but I decided to spend the weekend at my dad's place even though it wasn't my weekend to be there. Okay, so maybe that doesn't sound crazy. But try this: the reason I wanted to stay at my dad's is that I was hoping I would see Nick. I couldn't help it. No matter how hard I tried, no matter how he acted around me, I couldn't stop thinking about him. My stomach was full of butterflies as I rounded the corner onto my father's street—where I got the surprise of a lifetime.

Ben was standing outside my dad's building, his hands shoved deep into his jacket pockets, his shoulders rounded against the chilly wind that was sweeping the city. He straightened up when he saw me, but he didn't come toward me. Instead, he waited for me to approach him.

I hadn't seen or talked to Ben since I had told him that I was sorry—really sorry—but I couldn't go out with him anymore. He hadn't been particularly surprised by my announcement—he knew how I felt about Nick—but he still seemed to be crushed. He'd asked me if I was sure. I said yes. He asked me if I wanted some time to think it over. I had to say, no, I already had. I said, again, that I was sorry. I had never broken up with anyone before. It was a lot harder than I expected. And here he was again.

He looked terrific.

Ben is tall and athletic. He was wearing faded jeans and a well-worn jacket. That was one of the things I liked about Ben. He was casual even though he could afford to be flashy. His dad was extremely wealthy. Ben lived in one of the most exclusive neighborhoods in the city and went to the most exclusive private school.

"Hey, Robyn," he said.

"Hi, Ben." I'd forgotten how green and piercing his

eyes were. He was looking at me intently, as if he were trying to memorize me for a test.

"I went to see Billy," he said. "I also went to the police and told them where Billy was the day that guy Sean had the accident on the ice. I don't know if it will help, but I figured it was the least I could do."

Good old Ben. He always did the right thing. He was so responsible and reliable. That was why I had been attracted to him in the first place—because he was the exact opposite of Nick. It had taken me a while to realize that the exact opposite wasn't what I wanted.

"Billy said you'd been to see him a couple of times. I think it means a lot to him, Robyn."

I bristled at that. He made it sound as if he were Billy's best friend, as if he knew Billy better than I did.

He stepped closer to me. "I can't stop thinking about you, Robyn. I miss you."

"Ben, I—"

The door to my dad's building opened, and out came one large black dog followed by one tall young man dressed from head to toe in black.

Nick looked at me first, and for a moment I thought he was going to smile. Then Orion growled, and Nick's eyes shifted to Ben. The two of them stared at each other, and I knew they were both thinking the same thing: What is he doing here? Nick's expression hardened. He pushed by us.

Ben watched him disappear around a corner before he turned to me and said, "Are you seeing him again?"

"He lives here," I said.

"So that's it, then," he said stiffly.

"Ben, I'm sorry—"

"Right." He looked at me for a moment longer, as if there was something else he wanted to say. But in the end, he wheeled around and walked away without a word.

I stood there on the pavement, feeling bad for hurting him again and feeling worse remembering the expression on Nick's face. I wondered where he had been heading. I wondered if I should try to find him, maybe try to explain. I wondered what he would say if I did. If it would make any difference.

My cell phone rang. It was Morgan.

"He called me a puck bunny!" She was yelling so loudly that I had to hold the phone away from my ear. "Matt didn't want to tell me. I think he was embarrassed."

"He should have been."

"Puck bunny!" Morgan said again, still yelling. I hoped she wasn't using her phone outside. People who scream into their cell phones out on the street always look crazy. "You know what else Sean said? He said that puck bunnies will do whatever a hockey star like him wants. Can you believe it? That's what he thought of me, Robyn. He thought all he had to do was crook his little finger and I'd do whatever he wanted."

I thought about the way Morgan used to melt every time Billy put his arm around her.

"Some guys, huh?" I said.

"No wonder Billy attacked him," Morgan said. "If I had heard him say that, I'd have smacked him one." I heard a long sigh. "Where are you?" she said. "Can I come over?"

I told her where she could find me.

CHAPTER **TWELVE**

My dad wasn't home when I got upstairs. I tracked him down on his smartphone. He sounded surprised when he found out where I was.

"Did I mess up my schedule again?" he said.

"No. But Mom's working pretty much around the clock, so I thought—"

"It's okay, Robbie. You don't need an excuse to come over. Mi casa es su casa. But I won't be home until late."

"No problem, Dad. Morgan is coming over. We'll probably rent some movies or something."

Forty-five minutes later I buzzed in Morgan. She was breathless by the time she reached the third floor.

"You'll never guess who I just saw outside," she said between gasps. "Nick."

"I know," I said. "He lives here."

Morgan's eyes grew large. She peered around my father's enormous living space. "You mean here?" she said.

"I mean downstairs. My dad gave him back his old apartment."

Morgan eyed me cautiously. "So does that mean—"

"It means he's living downstairs," I said. "That's all."

"So you two aren't—"

I shook my head.

Morgan sighed. She kicked off her shoes, shrugged out of her jacket, and flopped down on one of the two large black leather sofas in my father's living room.

"I called Billy's mom," she said. "I told her that I want to go and see Billy. Robyn, she got all choked up when I said that. I think she was crying."

"She knows how Billy feels about you," I said. "He's miserable in there, Morgan. That's why he asked for that picture of the two of you that I took at New Year's."

Her face flushed. "And I tore it up."

"I had another copy at home. I gave him that one. But he knew right away that it wasn't his."

A little smile played across Morgan's lips. "I sort of signed the back of his copy."

"So I hear."

"Do you really think he didn't do it, Robyn?"

"I know he didn't."

"But the police—"

"The police think they have an open-and-shut case. They've got motive. They've got means. They've got his prints on the murder weapon. They've got him at the scene near the time Sean was killed."

"I heard your mom is his lawyer. At least that's good."

"Yeah. But it's not enough. Someone killed Sean, and it wasn't Billy. We have to find out who it was, Morgan. That's the only way Billy is going to be in the clear."

"How are we going to do that?"

"Well, you were pretty close to Sean in the last weeks of his life. What do you know about him?"

"That he was a jerk," Morgan said bitterly. "Except I didn't find that out until today."

"What else do you know about him?"

"Well, like Tamara said, he was competitive. His whole family is. You should see the house, Robyn. It's filled with trophies and framed press clippings going all the way back to when Sean and his brothers first started playing. Most of the stuff is Sean's, though. His mother has a scrapbook on him. It's this thick." She held her thumb and forefinger as far apart as they would go.

"Tamara said that he and Jon were rivals," I said. "Did Sean ever talk about him?"

"He said Jon was good at what he did."

"He said he was a good hockey player?"

"He said he was good muscle. But I got the feeling that he didn't respect Jon. He didn't think he was nearly as good a hockey player. Most enforcers aren't seen as star material." She sighed. "Sean really was good. If you read the clippings, Robyn, especially the recent ones, they all say the same thing—that he could be the next Great One. They say good things about Jon, too, but he doesn't get nearly as much mention as Sean."

"Well, he's team captain now. Maybe that will help him get noticed."

"Do you think Jon had anything to do with what happened?"

"I talked to him," I said. "I asked him where he was that night."

"And?"

"He said he was walking around downtown. Alone."

"So, no alibi," Morgan said. "He's on the team. He had access to the locker room and the equipment. He could have tampered with Sean's helmet."

"Sean looked everywhere for that helmet before the game," I said. "Isn't that what Kevin said?"

"He said Sean tore the locker room apart."

"Do you know where that assistant coach found it?"

"It was jammed under one of the locker-room benches," Morgan said slowly, as if she were realizing for the first time that something was wrong. "That's what Sean told me. He said he was surprised he didn't see it there himself."

"Well," I said, "if Jon was responsible for it going missing in the first place, he must have had an accomplice. If it had been in the locker room before the game, Sean would have found it. And Jon never left the ice once the game started. So that means that someone else must have put Sean's helmet back in the locker room during the game."

"An accomplice?" Morgan said. "You mean two people are involved in Sean's murder?"

I thought back to the night of the hockey game. I thought about what had happened and what I had heard out in the parking lot when I'd gone back to get my scarf. I remembered something else, too.

"I don't think anyone was trying to kill Sean that night," I said. "I think someone wanted him out of the game as badly as Jon did—but for a different reason." I looked at Morgan. "You know what we need to do? We need to talk to someone who knows what goes on in that arena—someone who sees who comes and goes."

"Wayne," Morgan said.

"The head janitor?"

She glanced at her watch.

"The arena's still open."

. . .

When we walked up to the front door of the arena, only a few lights were visible from the outside.

"It looks like it's closed. Are you sure Wayne is still here?" I said.

"That's his car," Morgan said, pointing to a beat-up white Camaro in the parking lot. "If it's here, he's here. And if he's here, the arena is open."

She led me around to the team entrance and pushed open the door.

"See?" She marched in as if she owned the place and called Wayne's name.

I looked around doubtfully. The place seemed deserted. There was no one on the ice. The stands were empty. The snack counter was dark.

"There's a light on in the players' locker room," Morgan said. "Maybe he's in there."

We were about to enter the locker room when someone burst out of it. We both jumped back, startled.

"Colin," Morgan gasped. "You scared me."

Colin Sloane looked as surprised as we were. He was carrying a plastic bag and a beat-up hockey stick.

"Morgan," he said. "What are you doing here?" He looked past Morgan at me and scowled. He was probably even more curious about why I was with her, especially since the last time he'd seen me, Morgan had frozen me out.

"We're looking for Wayne," Morgan said.

"He's in there." He gestured to the locker room door. "He found a few things of Sean's lying around. I came over to pick them up."

Morgan's expression softened. "That must have been tough," she said. "Are you okay, Colin?"

"Yeah." But he hadn't looked okay since the funeral. His jaw was set, like he was determined not to display any emotion, but his eyes gave him away. They were slightly unfocused, as if his mind were on what had been or might have been and not on the here and now. "If you want me to, Morgan, I'll wait for you. I'll drive you home."

Morgan's smile was gentle. "Thanks, Colin. But I'm with Robyn." She reached out and squeezed his hand.

Then she pushed the locker room door open. I followed her inside, where we found Wayne mopping the floor. His weathered faced brightened when he saw Morgan.

"Hi, Wayne," Morgan said. "You remember my friend Robyn?"

I nodded a hello. Wayne nodded back without taking his eyes off Morgan. Morgan got right to the point.

"Do you remember the day Sean's helmet came off?" she said.

"When someone tampered with it, you mean?" Wayne said.

Morgan nodded. "Did you see anyone go into or come out of the team locker room during the day or that evening before the team showed up?"

"With all the equipment in there, I keep the players' locker room locked before a game."

"But you're not the only person with a key, are you?" Morgan said.

"Coaches have keys."

"Does anyone else?" I asked.

Wayne shook his head.

"But I saw Sean unlock that door a couple of times," Morgan said.

Wayne shuffled uncomfortably. "Sometimes he borrowed the key from the board in my office. But that was okay with me. Sean was a good kid."

"What board?" I said.

"I have a board with hooks on it where I keep copies of all the keys for this place." I remembered seeing a board like the one he described the night of the hockey game, when I'd gone back to look for my scarf. "The originals are all right here." He jangled a ring that must have had fifty different keys attached to it.

"Did anyone besides Sean know about this board?" I said.

"Well, sure. Everyone who knows the arena knows my office and that board. But—"

"Do you always keep your office locked when you're not in it?"

Wayne shuffled uncomfortably again.

"So it's possible that someone could have taken the key from the board and gone into the players' locker room and tampered with Sean's helmet without you knowing it," I said.

"Everyone who knows the arena knows my office is off-limits," Wayne said.

I glanced at Morgan.

"Wayne, do you remember if anyone else was in the arena that day?" she said, her voice uncharacteristically gentle. "Anyone at all?"

"The place was real quiet," he said. "Besides the game that night, there was just the little-girl figure skaters after school. I had to prep the ice after they finished. That's it."

"Those were the only people in the arena before the game?" Morgan said. "Figure skaters?"

"Well, and some of the mothers. Some of them just drop the kids off. Some of them stay to watch."

Morgan gave me a look. I knew what she was thinking—it was highly unlikely that some junior figure skater's mother would tamper with Sean's hockey helmet.

"That's it?" Morgan said. "Little girls and their mothers?"

"And one dad. And Johnny," Wayne said.

"Johnny?" I said.

"Johnny Czerny," Wayne said. "His kid sister is in the figure skating class. His mom works, so he drops his sister off and picks her up. Sometimes he stays and watches."

"What about that day?"

Wayne's brow furrowed as he pondered the question. "He stayed."

So Jon had been at the arena the afternoon before the big game. Well, well.

"Did you see where he was? Was he in the stands watching the whole time?"

"The whole time?" Wayne said. "Well, I can't say. I saw him come in and I saw him and his sister leave together, but I didn't stay for the class. I have work to do around here. If you want to know what Johnny was doing that day, you'll have to ask him yourself."

I glanced at my watch. It was late.

"He'll be here first thing in the morning for practice," Wayne said.

"What time is first thing?" I asked.

"Six-thirty."

I was sorry I'd asked.

"Thanks, Wayne," Morgan said. She turned to go.

"Did you see anyone go into the locker room during the game that night?" I asked Wayne.

"No."

"You're sure?"

"Well . . ." he began. He frowned.

"What is it, Wayne?" Morgan said.

"There was one person," he said slowly. "I saw him go into the locker room during second period. When he came out, I asked him what he'd been doing in there. He said he was looking for some tape. He had some in his hand."

"Did you tell Sean's coach?" Morgan said.

"He was just looking for tape," Wayne said. "And he was an assistant coach."

"For Sean's team?"

"For the other team. But a coach would never tamper with equipment. A kid maybe. But not a coach. Coaches know what can happen when you monkey with equipment. They know how serious it can be."

"Do you know this assistant coach's name?" I said.

"Lyle something, I think," Wayne said. He thought it over. "Yeah. Lyle something."

"Thanks, Wayne," Morgan said. She pushed open the locker room door. "Colin?" I heard her say, surprised. "You're still here?"

"Are you sure I can't give you a lift?" he said. "It's no problem."

She stepped outside, and the door closed behind her. Wayne went back to his mopping.

"Can I ask you one more question, Wayne?" I said.

He glanced at me.

"You saw someone go into the arena the night Sean died, right?"

"Yeah. It was that kid, the one they arrested."

"Did you see him leave, too?"

"Couldn't have," Wayne said. "I wasn't here. I was on my way home when I saw him go in."

"But your car was in the parking lot when he left."

"No it wasn't. Like I told the cops, I saw the kid, I told him to remind Sean to lock up, and then I went straight home."

"Were there any other cars in the parking lot when you left?" I asked.

Wayne shook his head.

"You're sure?"

"Positive."

I thanked him and left the locker room. Something wasn't right. Billy had said he'd seen a car. He'd said it was Wayne's. But Wayne said it wasn't. Was he lying?

I found Morgan outside the locker room door.

"We're just trying to figure out a few things," she was saying to Colin.

"What things?" Colin said. "Why were you asking Wayne about the day of the game?"

"Because someone tampered with Sean's helmet," Morgan said.

"Yeah. The same creep they arrested for killing him. That psycho ex-boyfriend of yours." If you looked closely, you could see the resemblance between Sean and Colin. But that's all it was—a resemblance. Sean was tall, rangy, and handsome, with boyish good looks and a winning smile. Colin was stockier, beefier, with heavier features and, at that moment, a sullen scowl.

"Billy has an alibi for the whole day when Sean's helmet was tampered with," Morgan said.

"Are you trying to tell me he didn't kill Sean?" Colin said. "Because the cops said—"

"We're just saying that it looks like someone else besides Billy messed with Sean's helmet," I said.

"Yeah? So? What difference does that make now?"

"Maybe none," I said. On the other hand, maybe it would make all the difference in the world.

·   ·   ·

When I got home, I called the police homicide department and asked to speak to Charlie Hart. He sounded surprised to hear from me. His surprise turned to skepticism when I told him why I was calling.

"When did Billy tell you this?"

"A few days ago," I said. "He said it was the head janitor's car. But I just talked to the janitor, and he told me he went straight home. He also says he didn't see any other cars in the parking lot. So either he's lying, or someone pulled into the lot after he drove away and was still there when Billy left Sean in the arena. Maybe it was Sean's killer."

I didn't get the reaction I had hoped for.

All he said was, "Thanks for calling, Robyn."

It wasn't until I told my dad about it that I understood Charlie Hart's apparent lack of enthusiasm.

"It sounds like Billy didn't tell him what he told you. If that's true, then Charlie is probably wondering why Billy told you something just a few days ago that he never mentioned to the police at all," my dad said.

"But why would Billy lie about seeing a car in the parking lot?"

"Maybe he wants the police to think someone else went into the arena after he left."

"What if someone really did?"

"Who?" my dad said. "What motive did that person have for killing Sean Sloane? And how did the murder weapon end up in Billy's backyard?" When he saw the look on my face, he added quickly, "I'm not saying that Billy is lying, Robbie. I'm just saying, if I were on that case, those are the questions I would have."

"Would you follow it up?"

"Definitely. A good cop follows everything up."

.   .   .

I expected to be waiting alone at the arena for Jon Czerny first thing the next morning. Sure, Morgan had said she was going to be there. But Morgan is not a morning person. At least not a cheerful morning person. So I was stunned to find her already pacing in front of the main doors when I arrived. She was holding an extra-large latte and, judging from how frenetic she was, she must have almost finished it.

"I thought you weren't going to show up," she said.

I glanced at my watch. It was only quarter after six. "How did you get here so early, Morgan?"

"Colin drove me."

"Colin Sloane?"

"He called me last night after I got home. He's been calling me a lot since . . . well, you know. Mostly we talk about Sean. He's really broken up about what happened. I've been waiting for you since six."

"But Wayne said practice doesn't start until six-thirty."

Morgan rolled her eyes. "Don't you know anything about hockey?"

"No," I admitted. "And neither did you until you met Sean."

"They're supposed to be on the ice at six-thirty. They have to get all their gear on first," Morgan said. "Most of the team has already arrived." Her eyes skipped to some place behind me. "There he is."

Sure enough, Jon was striding across the parking lot toward the team entrance. Morgan and I started toward him. He smiled when he saw me and spit out the gum he was chewing. Then, like a blur, someone charged at him. It was Colin. He tackled Jon to the pavement and started punching him.

"Colin," Morgan screamed. "Stop!"

I ran toward the two of them and tried to pull Colin off Jon. Bad move. When I grabbed Colin's arm—his left one, it turned out—he lashed out with his right. He caught me right below the eye. The force of the blow sent me reeling, and I hit the pavement with a thud. I looked around for Morgan. Correction, I tried to look for Morgan, but both my eyes were blinded by tears and one of them, the one Colin had punched, was starting to swell shut. I could hear Colin pounding away at Jon.

"You tampered with my brother's helmet," he said. "You could have killed him."

I forced my good eye open. Jon was on his hands and knees, struggling to get up, but Colin kicked him in the ribs. Jon collapsed. As Colin drew his leg back to kick him again, Jon groaned and rolled into a ball. He protected his head and neck as best he could with his hands and arms. Morgan had vanished.

I staggered to my feet. I knew it was foolish to wade into the middle of a fight—again. But this wasn't really a fight. It was a beating. And that's exactly why I felt compelled to do something. I lurched toward Colin.

Just then the team entrance burst open and Morgan flew out. Two coaches and a couple of players followed her. They stopped for a split second to assess the situation. Then the coaches raced toward Colin and grabbed him by the arms. It took both of them to haul him away from Jon. A couple of players took over for one of the coaches, who knelt down to examine Jon. Colin was really worked up. He kept trying to break free so that he could charge at Jon again.

"He's the one," he said. "He tampered with Sean's helmet. It was him."

The coach kneeling next to Jon turned to the coach who was still working to restrain Colin.

"Call an ambulance," he said. "And the police. And get him," he pointed at Colin, "inside and sit on him until the police get here."

The second coach and the players had to drag Colin inside.

Morgan came over to me.

"Are you okay?" she said.

The coach who was kneeling beside Jon glanced up at me. "What happened to you?" he said.

"She tried to break up the fight," Morgan said.

Jon moaned.

The coach said, "How do you feel, son?"

Jon murmured something that I didn't hear.

The coach stood up and came to where I was leaning unsteadily against Morgan. I had never been punched in the face before. Not only did it hurt—really hurt—but it was scary. I couldn't believe that someone had actually hit me—hard enough that I'd been knocked off my feet. Hard enough that the very last thing that I wanted was to be hit ever again. I was trembling all over.

The coach took me gently by the chin and tilted my face up so that he could get a good look at me.

"You're going to have a real shiner," he said. "We should get you looked at, make sure there's no damage to your eye." He glanced at Morgan. "Take her inside and see if Wayne can find some ice. Make her sit down until the ambulance gets here."

Morgan took me by the elbow and steered me into the arena. I balked just inside the door when I saw Colin, flanked by a couple of players and being watched over by the second coach. His eyes met mine, but I didn't read any regret in them, only rage.

The ambulance came. So did the police. The two responding officers talked to Morgan and then to me. They spoke briefly to Jon after the paramedics had examined him and were getting ready to lift him into the ambulance. I heard one of them tell the police that they would have to take Jon to the hospital to see if anything was broken and whether he had a concussion. They'd probably keep him in overnight for observation. He also said that Jon was lucky—people don't realize how much damage kicking can do—and that he'd been smart to protect his head and neck. He told me that I should go to the hospital and get checked out too.

After the ambulance took Jon away and the officers had put Colin into the back of their car, one of the coaches, the one who had stayed with Jon, offered to drive me to the hospital. Morgan came too. When we got there, the coach started to come inside with us, but Morgan said it was okay, she would stay with me. She said that she would call my parents.

"Don't," I said as soon as the coach had left. "If you call my mom, she'll freak."

"What about your dad?"

"He left before I did. He'll be out of town all day. With any luck, I'll be in bed before he gets home." That way I wouldn't have to explain anything to anyone until tomorrow morning.

I was sent for an X-ray. After that, we waited almost an hour before a doctor examined me. All he said was, "You're going to have one heck of a bruise." He told me what to do for the swelling and prescribed some extra-strength painkillers.

"Come on," Morgan said. "I'll go home with you."

"What happened to Jon?" I said.

"I think they admitted him."

"We still need to talk to him."

"Are you sure you're up to it, Robyn?"

My face was throbbing, and I had a monster headache. But we were already there . . .

We asked at the information desk and were told that Jon was on the third floor. We found him lying in bed, facing the window. He was alone. Morgan and I looked at each other. I knocked softly on the doorframe. When Jon turned his head to look at us, I gasped. There were cuts on both cheeks. One eye was swollen shut. There was a nasty bruise on his forehead.

"That bad, huh?" he said, reading my expression. "You don't look so good yourself." The words came out slowly, as if he were having trouble shaping them. "The cops said you tried to pull him off me. Thanks." He tried to smile. It came out lopsided.

"I have to ask you something, Jon," I said.

He nodded.

"It's about Sean's helmet. You tampered with it, didn't you?"

His lopsided smile turned into a crooked scowl.

"Says who?"

"We know it was you," Morgan said, her voice shrill. "We know—"

I touched her arm to silence her.

"You usually back Sean up on the ice." I spoke calmly and hoped that he would listen. "That's your job. But the night Sean was hurt, you took a penalty for something stupid—right after the assistant coach found Sean's helmet. You knew how Sean was about his equipment. You knew he'd make them keep looking for his helmet until they found it. And as soon as they did, you provoked the other team by tripping one of their players for no reason. With you out of the game, you knew they'd go after Sean. You knew he'd end up either on the boards or in a fight—and with his helmet sabotaged . . ." I stared at him. "You wanted him out of the way, didn't you, Jon?"

No answer.

"One of the assistant coaches on the other team helped you. Wayne saw him go into the locker room right before Sean's helmet was found. What did you do, Jon? Did you make some kind of deal with him?" I remembered the angry voices I had heard in the parking lot. "Was your team supposed to lose? Was that it? But you didn't lose. You double-crossed your accomplice—and he didn't like that. That's why he threatened to go to the league and tell them what you'd done."

Jon's already pale face turned ashen.

Morgan stared at me, a stunned expression on her face.

"You never told me that," she said.

"I haven't said anything to the police yet, Jon," I said. "But I bet Colin has. They'll talk to Wayne, and then they'll talk to Lyle."

As soon as I mentioned the name Lyle, Jon sagged.

"You were in the arena before the game, watching your sister's skating practice," I said. "You know where Wayne keeps his duplicate keys. You could easily have taken Sean's helmet. And once the police find out about that, they'll start to wonder about some other things."

"Yeah," Morgan said. "Like where you were the night Sean was killed."

Sparks appeared in Jon's eyes. "What are you talking about?" he said. "You think I killed Sean?"

"You messed with his helmet," I said.

He stared at me for a moment before finally nodding.

"You wanted to get even with him," I said. "Because you were supposed to be team captain, but you were passed over in favor of Sean. And because he was attracting all the attention."

"I did it because he was a jerk," Jon said. "Because after he was named captain, he never let me forget it. He thought being captain gave him the right to boss me around. Bully me into taking chances the way he used bully Colin when Colin was backing him up—like he thought I should be happy to take a few concussions for him. And because he took credit for everything. Yeah, I know, the way he acts for the press and in front of the coaches. Perfect Sean Sloane. But when no one was looking—that was a different story."

"So you sabotaged him."

"Lyle asked me."

"But why?" I said. "He's a coach. I didn't think coaches did stuff like that."

"He's an assistant coach," Jon said. "And he's coaching because he's a washed-up player. Thanks to Colin Sloane. Colin hurt him bad two years ago. He can't play again—ever. He hates the whole Sloane family. He knew how I felt. He thought I'd help him take Sean out."

"And you did."

"I helped myself," Jon said. "If Sean was out for a few games, even the rest of the season, it would be good for me. It probably wouldn't even hurt his chances for NCAA. He and his mom had already visited a couple of campuses. He had plenty of opportunities."

"But I heard Lyle say something about a double-cross."

Jon shrugged. "I wasn't going to throw the game. I'd never do that. But if Lyle thought I would, well, that was

159

his problem. What could he do—report me? He was in it as much as I was. I just wanted Sean out of the way for the playoffs."

"And when it looked like that wasn't going to work, you got him out of the way permanently," Morgan said grimly. "I hope they lock you up forever."

"I didn't kill him."

"You have no alibi for the night he was killed," Morgan said.

"I was nowhere near the arena." His eyes were blazing now. "I didn't do anything."

"You told me you were downtown by yourself, Jon," I reminded him. "Can anyone back you up on that?"

He laughed. At least, he tried to. "Who do you think you are, the cops?"

"No. But I can always call them. They'll probably have a lot of questions for you when they find out you were the one who tampered with Sean's helmet."

"I am calling them," Morgan said. "I'm calling that detective—what's his name, Robyn?"

"Charlie Hart."

"I'm telling him that there was someone else who had a motive for killing Sean—someone who had already tried to kill him once at the hockey game."

"I wasn't trying to kill him."

"If he'd hit the ice harder when that player dropped his gloves that night, it could have been serious," Morgan said. "He could have died, and it would have been your fault."

"Morgan—" I said.

She was as sure now about Jon being the killer as she had been about Billy. And when Morgan was sure of something, there was no stopping her.

"But, Robyn, he just confessed—"

"Wait for me outside, Morgan, okay?"

"But—"

"Please?" I said.

She glowered at Jon and then at me. But in the end she nodded stiffly and went out in the hall to wait. I turned back to Jon.

"You said you were downtown. Where exactly were you?"

He shrugged and then winced from the pain. "Just around," he said. "I was angry—at Sean. Trying to clear my head."

"Did you see anyone?"

"No. I didn't want to see anyone. I wanted to be alone. I wound up in that old factory area by the water. It's quiet down there."

"And no one saw you?"

"I don't know. I don't think so."

"So why should I believe you, Jon?"

"I don't know. I don't care." He sounded angry and frustrated. "I didn't kill Sean."

He wasn't acting like a guilty person. He'd given no thought to an alibi. He clearly didn't think he'd need one.

"The cops are going to ask, Jon. They're going to want to check out where you were."

"Well, good luck to them. I was trying to get away from people, not be around them. The place was deserted except for whoever was in that old flour mill. But no one came out, at least that I could see, and I didn't go in."

"The old flour mill?" I said.

"Yeah. That big building. Yellow brick."

"People were in there?"

"Yeah," he said again, impatient. "I saw a lot of lights and I heard music, so I walked over. Something was going on in there. I listened for a while. I thought maybe it was a movie shoot or something."

"What time was this?"

"I don't know. Ten thirty. Eleven."

"Tell me exactly what you saw and heard."

He thought for a moment before telling me everything he could remember.

"Okay," I said when he had finished.

"Okay?" He sounded surprised. "That's it? Now what? Are you going to call the cops on me?"

"No. But I don't think Colin is going to keep quiet, so the police will probably want to talk to you about screwing with Sean's helmet."

"I'll probably get suspended from the league. I shouldn't have done it. I shouldn't have listened to Lyle. But—" He shook his head. "You didn't know Sean."

No, I didn't. And I was glad. He didn't sound like the nice guy I'd heard he was.

·   ·   ·

"You what?" Morgan said when I joined her in the hall. "He admitted that he tampered with Sean's helmet. He admitted that he wanted to get even with Sean. He admitted that he wanted him out of the way. And you actually believe his lame alibi?"

"It isn't lame," I said. "If he was where he says he was and if he saw what he says he saw, then it's actually pretty ironclad."

"Ironclad? He said he was walking around in a deserted part of town where nobody saw him."

I told her about my father's friend Hal and the new group he was managing. I told her about the top-secret music video shoot and that my dad had worked security on it.

"Nobody knew about it, Morgan. Nobody. But Jon did, which means he must have been there. And if he was there, there was no way that he could have been at the arena when Sean was killed."

Morgan looked doubtful. "Maybe he saw the video shoot before he killed Sean. Or after."

"I'm going to double-check," I assured her.

"Good," she said. "Because if it wasn't Tamara and it wasn't Jon, then who was it? Who killed Sean?"

Good question. But at least Morgan didn't regard Billy as the number-one suspect anymore.

CHAPTER THIRTEEN

Morgan came home with me. We had almost reached the second-floor landing when I heard the main security door open behind us. Morgan looked to see who it was.

"Oh," she said.

Nick was in the lobby. He stood there for a moment, looking up at me. I thought he was going to turn and leave the building. But he didn't. He frowned and started up the stairs.

"That looks bad, Robyn," he said, brushing past Morgan so that he could get a closer look at me. "Have you seen a doctor?"

I nodded.

"What happened?" he said.

"My dad has told me more than once that it's stupid to try to break up a fight unless you know what you're doing," I said. "It turns out he was right."

"You tried to break up a fight?"

"Dumb, huh?"

"You should put ice on that," he said.

"I will."

He looked into my eyes for a moment. It seemed like a heavenly eternity. Then he let go of me and started up the stairs ahead of us. I felt suddenly empty inside.

I glanced at Morgan. She just shook her head.

"Hey, Nick," I said.

He turned.

"You were out at that video shoot with my dad, right?"

"Yeah. Why?"

"There's this guy who says he was walking around near the old flour mill. He says he saw lights and heard music." I described exactly what Jon said he had seen and heard—and when. "Does that sound right to you?"

"It sounds dead-on."

"Is there any way he could have found out about the shoot from someone?"

"Not that I know of," Nick said. "And even if he did, it would have been hard to describe it with as much detail as he gave you. Why?"

"Just wondering."

"You're trying to help Billy, huh?"

"We both are," Morgan said.

Nick glanced at her and then turned back to me.

"This fight you tried to break up, did that have something to do with Billy, too?"

I nodded.

"He's a lucky guy to have a friend like you," Nick said.

He stared at me with his purple-blue eyes. I longed to slip my arms around him and to have him pull me close. That's when I blurted it out: "Ben and I broke up." I hadn't planned to say it. But I had imagined myself telling him. Plenty of times. And I had imagined what his reaction would be. Mostly I had imagined him smiling at me and picking me up and whirling me around and telling me how glad he was.

But he didn't do any of that. He didn't smile. He didn't pick me up. He didn't whirl me around. He just said, "You'd better put some ice on your eye, Robyn. And stay away from fights, okay?" He continued up to the second floor and disappeared through the door. Morgan and I climbed up to the third floor. Morgan went into the kitchen to get some ice and a clean towel. I tried not to cry. Tried, but didn't succeed.

.   .   .

Morgan's phone rang while I was icing my eye. She spoke to the caller for a few moments. When she hung up, I said, "That was Colin, wasn't it?"

"They arrested him for assaulting Jon, but they let him go with a warning. He said that Jon doesn't want to press charges. Colin apologized to him."

I hesitated a moment before asking her something that had been on my mind for a few days.

"Morgan, are you and Colin . . ." I couldn't make myself say it. I was afraid what the answer might be.

Morgan frowned. "Are we what?"

"He had his arm around you at the funeral. I saw you sitting with him in the cafeteria. He had his arm over the back of your chair. He drove you to the restaurant to meet Tamara and to the arena this morning. So I was wondering . . ."

"We're just friends," Morgan said. "Colin is really broken up about what happened to Sean. He feels responsible because he was supposed to pick Sean up that night."

"I heard his mom at the funeral. It sounded like she blames him for what happened."

"She was pretty upset," Morgan said. "Sean was the baby of the family. The way she treated him, it was pretty obvious that he was her favorite. Before she left the house the night Sean was killed, I heard her talking to Colin on the phone. She told him to make sure he picked Sean up. She didn't want Sean to go to the arena at all because of what had happened the night before, but Sean charmed her into it—as usual."

"So why didn't Colin pick him up?"

"He said he would. He was going to swing by the arena after he did some errands. But he finished those sooner than he expected and he didn't want to drive all the way home and then have to go back to the arena. So he pulled over. He said he was tired—he just closed his eyes for a couple of minutes. The next thing he knew, it was nearly morning. Can you imagine how he must have felt when he got home and found out what had happened to Sean?"

I couldn't.

"He asked me out," Morgan said.

"Who?"

"Colin. He asked me out—before I started going with Sean."

"You never told me that."

She shrugged. "I was with Billy then. Besides, I thought Colin was too much of a jock. And you know what I think of jocks."

"I thought I did," I said.

"It turns out he's not so bad. I kind of feel sorry for him."

"Because of what happened the night Sean died?"

"Because he got sidelined," she said. "He wanted to play hockey as much as Sean did. But he got injured. On top of that, he's been doing really badly at school. His mom is always on his case. Can you imagine what it's like being in some of the same classes as your little brother? And to have to watch him on the ice while you're waiting to see if you'll ever be able to play again?"

"What do you mean, ever?"

"Colin wants to get back into the major juniors. But you heard what Tamara said. After three concussions, he needs to get a medical clearance first."

"Do you think he'll get one?"

"I don't know," Morgan said. "I hope so."

. . .

I took some painkillers and prayed that my face would stop throbbing. Then we made a pot of tea. While we drank it, Morgan said, "I talked to Billy last night. I'm going with his mom to see him tomorrow."

"That's great," I said.

Or maybe not. Morgan stunned me by bursting into tears.

"What's the matter?" I said. "Is Billy okay? Did something happen to him?"

"He told me he loves me," she said.

"That's great." Except for the fact that she was crying. "Isn't it, Morgan?"

"After everything I said to Billy, after everything I did—oh, Robyn, after everything I thought, he still loves me." She sobbed.

I grabbed a box of tissues from the kitchen counter and led her to a sofa in the living room.

"Well, you know Billy," I said, handing her the tissue box. "He's a sweet guy."

"I know. But you can't believe what I said about him." She sobbed even harder.

I waited until she calmed down a little before speaking. "Billy asked me if you thought he did it."

She caught her breath. "What did you tell him?"

"I said that you know him better than almost anybody else. I said you know what kind of person he is."

"You didn't tell him what I said?"

I shook my head.

"Even after the way I treated you? Even after I was such a . . . a . . ."

"Bitch?" I said helpfully.

She nodded tearfully.

"I was thinking of Billy," I said. "Besides, I knew you'd come around sooner or later. Billy isn't a murderer. His biggest character flaw is that he loves you." I meant it as a joke, but it didn't make her laugh. Instead, it prompted another eruption of tears. I sighed and waited for her to calm down.

"I made a big mistake, Robyn," she said, dabbing at her eyes with a sodden wad of tissue. "I never should have dumped Billy."

"Why did you?" I asked. "What happened, Morgan? Did you just suddenly fall for Sean?"

"Yes," she said. Then, "No. I mean, that's not why it happened. I just—" She sighed. "You know Billy. He's always doing something good. Rescuing injured birds, helping homeless people, protesting abuse of animals."

"He's always been like that."

"I know. But he never expected me to be like that. It was always okay if I had different interests."

Like fashion. And shopping. Especially shopping.

"He started talking about volunteering at a wildlife rescue place that's just getting going. They want to get a sort of Habitat for Humanity project going to build the place. Billy thought it would be a fun thing for us to do. He said maybe we could spend some time there together. He said I'd learn all kinds of new things and that I'd really have fun."

"Maybe you would."

"No, I wouldn't. That's the thing. I don't want to build an animal shelter. I don't want to have anything to do with wildlife. Wild animals carry rabies and all kinds of other horrible diseases. They have sharp teeth. They're wild, Robyn."

"So you told Billy no?"

"I feel like I'm always telling him no. Or making excuses for why I can't do things with him. It's like we don't have anything in common."

"So you didn't like him anymore?"

"Didn't like him? I adored him, Robyn. He's sweet and funny and considerate. It's me. I'm the problem. I feel like a big fraud. I like leather boots, Robyn. I like chicken Caesars and BLTs. I like ice cream—the real kind, not the stuff made with soy or tofu. I love Missy." Missy was Morgan's dog. "But that doesn't mean I want to be a volunteer dog walker and pick up after dogs I don't even know. And dead birds?" She shuddered. "No way am I going to pick up a dead bird again—ever." DARC, Billy's bird-rescue group, picked up and counted birds that died after colliding with tall buildings.

"Did you and Billy have a fight? Is that it?"

"Not exactly."

"Then what?"

"I just—he made me feel bad." She looked at me. "No. That's not true. I did that all by myself. I felt guilty all the time. And then I met Sean—and he didn't care about anything except hockey and having fun, and . . . I'm a horrible person, aren't I? I dumped a guy who's practically a saint, and I got dazzled by a jock."

"You got dazzled by Sean Sloane, the object of every girl's desire." Well, almost every girl. He didn't do anything for me. "And from what I hear, he came on to you in a big way."

"The day after I first talked to him, he was waiting for me at my locker," she said. "At first I thought he was waiting for someone else. But he smiled at me and stepped aside for me when I got there, and I thought, Wow, he knows it's my locker. Sean Sloane actually knows which locker is mine."

"I didn't know you were so impressed by him in the first place," I said. "You never mentioned him before, and he's a *huge* jock."

"I know," she said, embarrassed. "But Sean—he was so hot, Robyn. Everyone thought so. I just never thought he would be interested in me. I mean, he had a girlfriend. And he was a senior. But that doesn't mean I didn't notice him. No way. And then one day there he was, stepping aside so that I could open my locker. He watched me while I got my stuff out. Then, when I closed my locker, he said, 'Aren't you even going to say hi?' So I did. And the next thing I knew, he was walking me to class and telling me he'd been noticing me a lot in the halls. He said he liked the way I moved. He asked if I was a model."

I groaned.

Morgan's face flushed. "I know," she said. "Can you think of a lamer line? But I fell for it. I was actually flattered. And it just kind of escalated from there."

"It's not your fault," I said. "He was out to get you. He wanted to get even with Tamara—and with Billy."

"I feel like such an idiot. How could I have fallen for him?"

"It sounds like you didn't fall for him. You fell for the fact that he was different from Billy—and for his image," I said. "You weren't the only one, Morgan. He had a ton of fans. Everyone seemed to like Sean." I was beginning to think that the emphasis should be on the word *seemed*. "He had all kinds of friends—from other jocks like him to nerds like Aaron Arthurs."

"Aaron Arthurs?" Morgan looked at me as if I were crazy. "Where did you get the idea that Sean was friends with Aaron?"

"Aaron knows Sean's locker combination. He lent Sean textbooks when Sean lost his or forgot them at home."

"Aaron knew Sean's locker combination?"

"I saw him open Sean's locker. He was taking his books back. Why? Weren't they friends?"

"Not that I know of. Sean mentioned him a few times, but only to put him down."

"Well, Aaron seemed to think they were friends," I said. "So there you go. You weren't the only person to be fooled by him."

"If that's supposed to make me feel better, it doesn't," Morgan said. "No matter how you look at it, I fell for a guy who turns out to be nothing like what I thought he was. What does that say for my ability to judge character? What does it say about *my* character? I mean, I know I'm not Billy, but how superficial do you have to be to fall for an image instead of a real person?"

"People do it all the time, Morgan. That's what sells all those gossip magazines."

"Maybe. But I should have known he wasn't everything he was cracked up to be. When he found out that I was an A student, he started asking me for help with his homework."

I remembered her in the library doing a biology assignment for him.

"But he was getting good grades," I said. "Why did he need help?"

"He said it was a time thing mostly. He had so many games and practices. And he was always putting in extra time on the ice. Whatever else he was, he was dead serious about hockey. He wanted to be the best. But sometimes that meant he didn't have time to do all his homework. So . . ." She hung her head. "I bailed him out a couple of times."

"You did his homework for him?"

She nodded. She looked thoroughly ashamed.

"The first time, I didn't see anything wrong with it. I mean, like you said, he was getting good grades. He could have done it himself—he just ran out of time."

"Seems reasonable."

"The thing is . . ." She hesitated. "He asked me to do some math homework for him one time. When I didn't get around to it, he got mad at me. So I said, you've got time now. Let's go to the library. I have work to do. You can do your math. But he said I'd promised to do it and a promise is a promise. I told him I was sorry, but he got really worked up. He said he didn't realize I was the kind of person who broke promises. He was really angry. So . . . I caved. I did his homework for him with him just sitting there watching me. And . . . I don't know, I just had this feeling. So I started screwing it up, you know, making mistakes on purpose while he was watching me. And you know what, Robyn? He didn't even notice."

"You mean, he was distracted?"

"I mean, I don't think he understood what I was doing. Anyway, he backed off after that and stopped asking for my help."

"That doesn't make sense," I said. "You said it yourself—he was getting good grades. He had to if he wanted to keep playing hockey. He was going to use his grades to convince his mom that he'd still be able to go to college later if his hockey career didn't work out."

"I know what I said. I also know what I saw. If you ask me, Sean was cut out for hockey, not college."

"Did you help him a lot, Morgan?"

She nodded slowly. "It was getting so I was spending more time on his homework than on mine. I spent a whole night doing an English project for him while he was at the arena practicing. He called me that night at midnight, after he got home, to make sure I e-mailed the assignment to him so he could hand it in on time."

"It didn't bother you?"

"To be honest," she said, "I felt funny about it. But every time I decided to talk to him about it, he'd say something incredibly sweet or he'd start hugging me and, well, you know." She let out a long, shuddery sigh. "I can't believe I fell for him. I can't believe I let him touch me."

We were silent for a few moments. Then, at exactly the same time, we looked at each other and I swear we both had the same thought.

"If you were doing his homework for him for the past couple of weeks," I said, "who was doing it before you?"

CHAPTER **FOURTEEN**

Hotshot, up-and-coming, popular, smart Sean Sloane.

Sean Sloane, who was turning out not to be as nice as a lot of people thought he was—at least, according to Tamara Sanders and Jon Czerny.

Sean Sloane, who was turning out to be not as smart as everyone thought he was—at least, according to Morgan.

Sean Sloane, who, it seemed, was determined to get ahead and didn't care how he did it. He had taken advantage of the publicity Tamara had been able to generate for him but had turned spiteful when he found out she was cheating on him. He had knocked Jon Czerny out of the team-captain spot. He had used Morgan to get back at both Tamara and Billy—for something that, in Billy's case, had happened years earlier. He had even gotten Morgan to do his homework for him. Had he done his own work before then? Or had he charmed someone else into doing it for him?

I looked up the number of the TV station where Tamara worked and ended up leaving a message on her voice mail. She called me back within the hour.

"Academically?" she said in response to my question. "He did okay, I guess."

"Did you ever help him with assignments?"

"We used to do homework together," she said. "And, yeah, sometimes when he was jammed for time I bailed him out. But that goes back at least a year. After I got my part-time job at the station, I didn't have as much time. I had enough trouble getting my own work done. Why?"

"I was just wondering," I said.

"Sean was a smart guy," she said. "He just had his priorities, you know?"

And priority number one was Sean Sloane.

"Morgan," I said after I hung up. "Do you think Colin would let us look at the computer he, Sean, and Kevin shared?"

"We can ask him," Morgan said. "Come on. He's at home."

.   .   .

Colin stood in the open doorway, staring at my black eye.

"I felt someone grab me," he said. "I didn't know it was you. Is your eye okay?"

"No permanent damage," I said.

"Sorry."

I glanced at Morgan.

"We need your help, Colin," she said. She explained what we wanted.

"I don't know," Colin said slowly. "My mom's upstairs sleeping."

"We'll be quiet," Morgan said.

Still Colin hesitated.

"I don't get it," he said. "What are you up to? The cops have the guy who did it."

"Please, Colin?" Morgan said, making her large eyes even larger and cranking her pouty charm up to maximum. "You're probably right." I stared at her. Did she really mean that? Did she still have doubts about Billy? "But Robyn and I have known Billy since we were kids. I'm just trying to understand what happened."

Colin peered down into her eyes, and his face softened.

"Okay," he said reluctantly. "But you have to be really quiet. I'm not kidding."

Morgan promised for both of us, and we followed Colin up the stairs to Sean's room. When he pushed open the door, Morgan stifled a gasp.

"Nothing's changed," she said softly. The room was filled with hockey trophies, hockey posters, photos of Sean in full hockey gear—hockey, hockey, hockey.

Sitting on a desk near the window was a computer.

"Is it okay if I turn it on?" I said.

Colin shrugged.

When it booted up, it prompted me for a password. I turned to Colin, who merely shrugged again.

"But you and Sean shared the computer, didn't you?" I said. "Kevin, too. That's what Sean told Mr. Dormer when his locker was trashed. He said that's why he didn't keep any of his essays on the hard drive—because you and Kevin always fooled with his stuff."

Colin looked down at the floor for a moment. I remembered that he had done the same thing when Sean had looked to him for confirmation the day his locker was trashed.

"He lied to Mr. Dormer, didn't he, Colin?" I said.

It took a moment, but he finally nodded. He looked at me.

"He never let anyone touch his computer."

"Why would he lie?" Morgan said.

"Do you know if he wrote down his password anywhere, Colin?" I said.

Colin shook his head.

"Great," I muttered. I glanced around the room again. There were at least a dozen full-color hockey posters on the wall. The only one I recognized was Wayne Gretzky. It was worth a try. I turned back to the computer, typed in *Gretzky*—and got an error message. I glanced at the posters again. "Who's that guy?" I asked Colin.

"You're kidding, right?" Morgan said. "Even I know him. That's Sidney Crosby."

"Show-off." I typed in Crosby's name—and got another error message. "So much for that. Anyone have any other ideas?"

Morgan shook her head. "It was either on or off when I was over here. I never saw him turn it on."

I looked at Colin, who was gazing at the posters.

"Try 'The Greatest One,'" he said. "That's how Sean always referred to himself."

I typed the words in. It worked.

First I looked at his documents. Despite what Sean had told Mr. Dormer when his locker was trashed, there were plenty of school documents on his hard drive. I clicked into his e-mail and poked around, scanning the inbox and the outbox.

"Well, well," I said.

Colin and Morgan leaned over my shoulder so that they could look at the screen.

"Can I print some of these?" I asked Colin. He shrugged.

"Does this mean what I think it means?" Morgan said.

"Come on," Colin said. "You think that guy killed Sean? No way."

I could see why he thought that. But if there's one thing I know, it's that you never know.

"Let's talk to him," Morgan said. "Let's find him and talk to him right now."

"We don't even know where he—"

"What are you doing in Sean's room?" a sharp voice said behind us.

I whirled around. Sean's mother was standing in the doorway. Her hair was wild. Her eyes were hollow. Her face was pale.

"Get out," she said. "Get. *Out*."

"Mom, you remember Morgan," Colin began.

His mother pushed past me. She grabbed Colin by the arm and started to push him out of the room.

"This is Sean's room," she said. "You know he doesn't like people in his room, especially when he isn't here."

"Mom, we were just—"

"Get out," she screamed. "You, of all people, get out!"

Colin stared at her. For a moment it looked like he was going to say something, but in the end he just turned and ran down the stairs. I heard a door slam at the bottom.

Morgan started after him. I followed. As I left the room, Sean's mother sank down on the bed. She took one of Sean's pillows, held it up to her face, and inhaled deeply.

We found Colin in the driveway, sitting in a navy blue Malibu that looked almost as old as I was. The rear bumper was decorated with hockey decals. A team pennant fluttered from a window fixture. Colin was in the driver's seat, pounding his fists against the steering wheel.

"It's my fault," he said, his voice muffled by the closed windows. "It's all my fault."

Morgan circled around to the passenger side and got in. I saw her lips moving, but I couldn't hear what she was saying. She touched Colin's arm and then tugged it gently so that he looked at her. Suddenly he flung his arms around her and held her tightly. I saw his shoulders heaving. Colin Sloane was crying. Morgan stared at me through the window. I know she felt sorry for him, but I think she also felt awkward. After a few moments, they separated and Morgan waved to me to get in. I climbed in the backseat of what turned out to be the messiest car I had ever been in. There were notebooks and paper all over the backseat. The floor was littered with empty pop cans and fast-food wrappers.

"I was just telling Colin that we're going to get to the bottom of this, no matter what," Morgan said. "We are, aren't we, Robyn?"

"What good will it do?" Colin said. "What good will anything do now? You saw my mom. What does it matter who killed Sean? Nothing is ever going to bring him back."

"It matters," Morgan said softly. "It matters that the police have the right person. It matters that the person pays for what he did."

"You can't pay for something like that," Colin said bitterly. "The damage is done. Paying doesn't change anything."

We sat there in silence for a few moments before Morgan reached for the door handle and said, "I want to find out what was going on. Maybe you don't see the point to it, Colin. But I do. I want to know who did it, and I want that person to be punished."

"Even if it turns out that the cops are right?" Colin said. "Even if it turns out to be that guy you used to go out with?"

Morgan glanced at me. "Even then," she said. "It matters to me, Colin. It should matter to you, too."

Colin was silent for a few moments. Then he turned the key in the ignition. "Where do we start?" he said.

.   .   .

I started with directory assistance and got connected to Aaron Arthurs's home phone. His mother answered.

"I'm sorry, Aaron isn't here," she said.

When I asked when she expected him, she offered me his cell number.

"Pen and paper," I said, fumbling in my purse. Morgan found a pen and handed it to me. I snatched up a crumpled piece of paper from the floor of Colin's car and scrawled the number that Aaron's mother gave me. Then she said, "If he doesn't answer, it's probably because he's at his club."

"Club?"

"His games club. They have a place over a butcher's store. It's cold and it smells, but they don't seem to care. They're always wrapped up in their games. They turn their phones off." She told me where the club was, and I scrawled that down, too.

When I told Morgan and Colin what I had found out, Morgan said, "Let's try the club first. I'd rather surprise him. That will give him less chance to make up any excuses. Or to dodge us."

I nodded.

"I'll take you there," Colin said.

. . .

Aaron definitely looked surprised when Morgan, Colin, and I walked into the room above a butcher shop that was, as advertised, cold and smelly. The rest of the room's occupants, all of them crowded around small tables on which were game boards and cards, looked equally startled to see strangers in their clubhouse.

"What are they playing?" Morgan said. She peered at the nearest games table.

"Some kind of role-playing game, I think," I said. For some reason, role-playing was hugely popular with guys like Aaron.

One of the players glowered at us.

"We're here to see Aaron," I said, my voice loud enough for Aaron to hear me.

Aaron stood up slowly and came over to the door. He looked apprehensively at Colin, who towered above him. Then he turned to me.

"We want to talk to you about Sean," I said.

"What's there to talk about?" He sounded cocky until he remembered that Sean's brother was standing right there. "I mean, the cops caught the guy who did it, right?"

"But they didn't catch the guy who trashed Sean's locker," I said.

Aaron laughed.

"What does that have to do with anything? He's dead." He glanced at Colin. "No offense." He turned back to me. "I mean, at this point, who cares about his locker?"

"The police will care," I said, "if it turns out whoever trashed his locker was angry enough to want him dead." I stared him right in the eye. "Were you, Aaron?"

"Was I what?"

"Angry enough to want Sean dead?"

"What? You think I trashed Sean's locker?" His eyes shifted to Morgan. "You told Dormer that your ex-boyfriend did it. You made a big deal about it."

"Billy didn't kill Sean," I said.

"Well, neither did I. Besides, the lock was cut off with a bolt-cutter. I didn't need a bolt-cutter to get into Sean's locker. I had the combination."

"Right," Morgan said. "Because you and Sean were such good friends—even though he made fun of you all the time."

Aaron's face turned red.

"You knew that, right?" Morgan said. "You can't believe the things he used to say about you to his buddies."

"Sean thought you were a geek," I said. "He made fun of you all the time. So why were you helping him cheat?"

Aaron glanced over his shoulder at his friends. They were all staring at us now.

"Can we step outside?" he said.

We moved into the hall. Aaron closed the door behind us.

I repeated my question.

"I don't know what you're talking about," Aaron said.

"Really?" I held out the sheaf of e-mails that I had printed at Sean's house. "This last one sounds kind of threatening. I'm guessing that you weren't helping him out of the goodness of your heart."

Aaron glanced at the e-mail. "That doesn't prove anything."

I read the e-mail out loud: "'Now you're on your own. I hope you fail every subject and lose your scholarship, you miserable creep.' It's dated two days before Sean's locker was trashed." I turned to Morgan and Colin. "What do you think?"

"I think we should take these e-mails to Mr. Dormer," Morgan said. "I think we should also tell him that Aaron is the one who broke into Sean's locker, shredded all of his notebooks and papers, and destroyed his flash drive."

"I already told you I didn't do that," Aaron said. "I had his locker combination. He gave it to me. If I wanted to get into his locker, all I had to do was open the lock."

"That's why you used a bolt-cutter," I said. "Sean knew you had his combination. I bet he let you have it so that you could leave his assignments for him—the ones that he had to copy out, like math homework. You'd leave it in the locker, right?" I held out another e-mail to prove it. "If someone had just opened his locker and destroyed everything, you'd have been the prime suspect. So you broke in instead."

"Yeah," Morgan said, her tone pure acid. "You knew Billy would be blamed."

"Why'd you do it?" I said. "Why did you trash Sean's stuff?"

Colin took a menacing step toward him. Aaron cringed.

"I didn't. I swear I didn't," he said.

"Then who did?"

"Sean."

"Right," Morgan said. "Sean trashed his own locker." She shook her head.

"He did," Aaron said. "You have to believe me."

"Why would Sean do something so stupid?" Morgan said.

"Because I told him I wasn't going to help him anymore. And because I didn't do the project he was supposed to hand in that day."

"You're lying," Colin said.

"Are you saying that Sean messed up his own locker because you didn't do a project for him?" I said.

"He didn't want to get in trouble," Aaron said. "Mr. Bruce made it pretty clear how he'd deal with late assignments."

I knew Mr. Bruce. He had a reputation. He did not tolerate tardiness. What Aaron was saying kind of made sense. I turned to Morgan. "That's why Sean lied about his computer. He said he didn't store assignments on it because his brothers kept screwing around with it. But that's not true." I glanced at Aaron. "Sean was trying to buy time."

"Yeah," Morgan said bitterly. "Time for me to do the work for him instead."

"He came up to me later that day and threatened me," Aaron said.

"Threatened you?"

"Is that why you killed him?" Morgan said. Colin took another step toward Aaron, who scuttled backward until he was plastered against the wall.

"I didn't kill him," he wailed.

"How did he threaten you?" I said. "What did he say?"

"That if I didn't do what I was told, he'd turn me in for helping him cheat."

"But that would hurt him just as much."

Aaron hung his head. "I did more than just doing homework for him," he said quietly.

"What do you mean?"

"The more I did for him, the more demanding he got. He also got lazy. He didn't want to have to study at all."

I remembered that Aaron had been startled when I'd walked in on him in the copy room at school. He had tried to hide what he was copying. Aaron was in the office all the time. He helped his mother after hours. He even did troubleshooting on the computer system from time to time.

"What else were you doing for him, Aaron?"

Aaron refused to look at me.

"Tell us, Aaron, or I'll go straight to Mr. Dormer on Monday and tell him everything I know. Then I'll go to the police. I hope you have an alibi for the night Sean was killed."

Aaron's face went white. "Okay," he said. He drew in a deep breath. "My mother does a lot of photocopying for teachers."

"That photocopying includes tests, doesn't it?" I said softly.

Aaron nodded again. "I'm not in any of Sean's classes. We don't even have any of the same teachers. So . . ."

"So nobody would suspect you of helping him cheat," I said.

He nodded.

"Sean had an e-mail from me about what I was doing," he said. "I actually offered to help him. I was flattered. He came up to me in the hall about a year ago and started talking to me." Tamara had told me that she had stopped helping Sean at about the same time. "He said he had some questions about physics and he asked me for help. He was really nice—you know, friendly, funny. Then, during the summer, he got me a job at the same place he worked, at one of those big hardware stores. We hung out together at lunch. When school started again, he told me he was worried about his grades. He asked me to tutor him. He offered to pay, but I said no, I didn't mind helping. I felt lucky—I'd be helping Sean Sloane!"

"So what happened?" I said. "Why did you stop?"

"At first it seemed like he really wanted to learn. Then he started skipping tutoring sessions—he said he had to practice. He also started bossing me around. He wasn't friendly anymore. And when I told him, forget it, I wasn't going to help him anymore, he told me I couldn't do that without getting myself into big trouble. He'd saved all my e-mails. He said he'd get into trouble, too, but probably not as much as me. After all, I had offered to help him. It always came out that way. He never asked—he always got me to offer."

"But you did try to stop," I said.

"Because I almost got caught. Mr. Dormer walked in on me in the copy room, just like you did. It really scared me—I told Sean I was through. That's when he trashed his own locker. He was furious. He told me he was going to admit he'd been accepting my help. He was going to say that he'd just found out that I was stealing tests for him—that he didn't know before, that he had no idea I was using actual test papers. He said they'd believe him, not me. He said people would wonder how long I had been cheating for, whether I'd really earned my grades." His eyes were watery. "Sean was going to turn me in. There was nothing I could do . . ."

"Except kill him," Morgan said.

"Except do what he wanted me to do," Aaron said. "I had to. He only had a couple more months in high school. So I caved. It was the only thing I could do."

"Where were you between ten and midnight the night Sean was murdered?" I said.

"At home."

"Right," Morgan said. "I don't suppose you have any witnesses?"

"No."

Morgan snorted. "That's a pretty weak alibi."

"Your parents weren't around?" I said.

Aaron shook his head. "They were out of town. My dad was at a convention. My mother went with him."

"You don't have any brothers or sisters?"

"Not living at home. My older brother's a grad student."

"Come on," Morgan said. "Let's call that detective."

"Come on. Look at me," Aaron said. "Do you think I'd have a chance against Sean?" Aaron was short, slight, and mousy-looking. It was hard to imagine that he could get the better of Sean physically.

"Sean was killed by a blow from behind," I said. "Whoever did it must have surprised him. You could have done that." Anyone angry enough could have picked up that piece of pipe. But that didn't mean just anyone would if given the chance. I looked at Aaron. He was trembling.

"I didn't kill him," he said.

"What kind of car do you drive?" I said.

"Car?" Aaron looked confused. "I don't have a car. I don't even have a driver's license."

I studied him for a few moments more. I could picture a lot of things, but I couldn't picture him killing Sean.

"Come on," I said to Morgan.

"Wait," Aaron said, his voice shrill. "Are you going to call the cops on me? I know what I did was wrong. But I didn't kill him. I swear I didn't. But he's dead—"

Colin made a menacing rumble. Aaron shrank back.

"If you call the police, I'll have to tell them Sean was cheating. His mom will find out. You don't want that, do you? It will only hurt her."

"Not to mention that it'll kill your chances at getting into college," I said. "Come on. Let's get out of here."

We left the club and went back to the car. Morgan got into the backseat and crossed her arms over her chest. Colin climbed in beside her. With a sigh, I got into the front passenger seat and turned to look at her. She scowled at me.

"You don't think he did it, do you?" she said.

"No," I said. "Look at him, Morgan. He's not the type."

"He had a motive."

"All he wants is get into Harvard or Yale or some-place like that."

"He doesn't have an alibi."

"That's another thing," I said. "He's a smart guy, Morgan. Don't you think if he killed someone, he'd come up with an alibi?"

"So what are you saying?" she said. "He didn't do it. Jon didn't do it. Tamara didn't do it. Who does that leave? Are you saying it was Billy?"

"Of course not." I dug in my pocket for my phone. The paper that I had written Aaron's cell number on fell out. I picked it up. Uh-oh. It wasn't a piece of scrap paper. I had written on the back of a letter. I skimmed it.

"Well, now what?" Morgan said impatiently.

"I'm going to call my mom. She'll know if the police have talked to Wayne. Or if they talked to Billy again."

"Wayne?" Colin said. "What does Wayne have to do with this?"

I told him what I knew: Billy had seen Wayne's car in the parking lot when he left the arena, but Wayne had told me he'd gone right home after seeing Billy.

"You think Wayne killed Sean?" Morgan said.

"That's crazy," Colin said.

"Everything's crazy," Morgan said. "It's crazy that Sean is dead. It's crazy that he was such a jerk. It's crazy that the police think that Billy did it. I wish I'd never talked to Sean." She got out of the car and slammed the door behind her.

Poor Morgan. She seemed to have given up hope. I couldn't blame her. We were getting nowhere.

Colin scrambled out after her. As I reached for the door handle to follow them, my phone rang.

It was Billy.

"Are you okay?" I said. "Where are you?"

CHAPTER FIFTEEN

"Where do you think I am?" Billy said. He sounded tired. "Your mom was just here with that detective. She arranged for them to let me call you. Can you come see me again, Robyn? Can you bring Morgan?"

"Charlie Hart was there?" I said. That was good. "What did he want?"

"He asked me about the car I saw in the parking lot when I left the arena. But I don't think he believed me."

"Did he say anything to you about the head janitor?"

"No." I wasn't surprised. Cops never talk about things like that. Especially not with someone they consider a suspect. "Why? What about him?"

"The janitor told me he left right after he saw you go into the arena. He said he went home. But you told me you saw his car in the parking lot. So that means he lied to me. I called Charlie Hart and told him. He said he'd look into it."

"So that's why he was here," Billy said. "He asked me about the car and why I hadn't mentioned it any of the times I talked to him."

"What did you tell him?"

"That I didn't say anything about it because I didn't know it was important. They told me someone saw me go into the arena. I saw the janitor—I spoke to him—so I knew who they meant. They didn't make a big deal about whether he saw me leave, so I didn't either."

"Did Detective Hart say anything today about whether he saw you leave?"

"He didn't say anything." There was an edge to his voice. "He just asked me to describe the car. So I did. And I could see right away that he didn't believe me."

I wondered why Charlie Hart wouldn't have believed him. Unless . . .

"What exactly did you tell him, Billy?"

"What does it matter?"

"Come on, Billy."

"That it was a dark-colored car, but I couldn't tell exactly what color. It was parked at the far end of the parking lot. Not under a light or anything."

"Dark-colored?" I said. Wayne drove a white Camaro—I'd had no trouble making out the color when Morgan and I had gone to the arena the night before. "Are you sure?"

"I know what I saw, Robyn."

"Did you see the license plate? Even part of it?"

"No."

"Do you remember anything else about it?"

"You sound like that cop," he said irritably.

The driver's-side door opened.

"Billy, the car you saw wasn't Wayne's," I said. "It belonged to someone else. Maybe someone who went into the arena right after you left."

"Well, tell that to your detective friend, because he didn't believe a word I said."

Colin climbed in behind the wheel. I glanced around. Morgan was nowhere in sight.

"What else do you remember about the car, Billy?" I said.

"Nothing. If I'd known it was going to be important, I would have memorized every detail. But it was just a car."

I glanced out the window again. Where was Morgan?

"Think, Billy. Can you tell me anything else about the car you saw? Anything at all?"

"It was dark, Robyn." There was a long pause at the other end of the line. "I think maybe there was a flag or something on the back of it."

"What do you mean, a flag?"

"I don't know. There was something sticking up from the back. A flag."

"From the back?" I said slowly. "Maybe from a rear window?"

Colin turned to look at me. His car had a hockey banner sticking up above the rear driver's-side window. I reached for the door handle as Billy said, "Yeah. Maybe from a rear window."

Colin grabbed the phone from my hand.

"Hey," I said.

He started the car. The lock *tchonked* down. I fumbled to open it, but by then the car was screeching away from the curb.

.   .   .

We didn't go far, but it seemed like the end of the earth when we got there. Colin pulled his car to a stop at the edge of some bluffs that towered high above the waterfront. Far below was a park and, beyond that, the water. On a warm spring or summer afternoon, the park would have been filled with cyclists, walkers, picnickers, and people walking their dogs. Motorboats would have been skimming across the lake. But at this time of year the park was deserted. Colin and I were the only people at the top of the bluffs.

I fumbled for the door handle again. Colin grabbed my wrist and wrenched it away.

"What are you doing?" I said. "Why are we here? Why won't you let me out?"

"I can't," he said. "I just can't."

"Morgan knows I'm with you."

"Morgan took off. She said she wanted to see her boyfriend."

"She'll know you were the last person to see me."

He stared sullenly out the windshield. His hand was like a vise around my wrist.

"Colin, you have to let me go."

Just like that, he let go. I unlocked the door, and this time Colin didn't try to stop me. He sat rigid in the driver's seat, staring out over the water below us. I hesitated.

"Go on," he said finally, without looking at me. "Get out."

But I couldn't make myself move. A hundred different thoughts were colliding in my brain—the car Billy had seen in the parking lot when he left the arena, the way the killer had covered Sean's face, what Morgan had told me about Colin, the letter I had found crumpled in the back seat of the car.

"What happened that night at the arena?" I said.

Colin slammed his fists against the steering wheel and let out a howl of anguish.

"He was my brother," he said. "It was my job to protect him. Take care of him. That's what my mother always taught us—the bigger ones take care of the little ones."

"Jon told me that you protected Sean on the ice," I said. "He said you kept Sean in the clear. You kept the goons away from him. He said that's why you were injured so often."

Colin was clutching the steering wheel as if it was the only thing keeping him in the car.

"Was it because of this?" I held up the piece of paper that I'd scrawled Aaron's cell number on. It was a letter from Colin's doctor, stating that Colin should not be allowed to play hockey again. The risk of another concussion was too great, and another concussion could prove fatal. "Was it because you weren't going to be able to play hockey anymore and everyone said Sean was going to go pro?"

"My dad played professional hockey," Colin said, still staring resolutely out the windshield. "Not for that long—two years. But he always said it was the best two years of his life. He said that nothing else even came close. He had us on skates practically before we could walk. First Kevin. Then me. Then Sean. But Sean was the best. Sean had real talent."

His knuckles were white against the dark covering of the steering wheel.

"Mr. Charm," he said. "That's what my mother used to call him. Everyone liked him. He could talk anyone into anything—Mom, his coaches, his teachers—anyone."

I didn't say anything.

"I went to pick him up, just like I promised Mom I would," he said. "I got there at ten—right on time. I saw that kid come out of the arena."

"Billy," I said.

Colin nodded. "Sean hated that kid—ever since peewee hockey. You have no idea how he could hold a grudge. Like an elephant. He never forgot. Never."

"Tamara said that was one of the reasons Sean started going out with Morgan," I said. "To get back at Billy."

Colin glanced at me. "She's so pretty," he said.

Morgan could turn heads, that was for sure.

"I asked her out a couple of times," he said.

"She told me."

"But she always turned me down."

I waited.

"When Sean found out that Tamara was cheating on him, he went nuts. He told her he wouldn't do the documentary she was planning, even though it would have been good for him. He said he didn't care. All he cared about was making sure Tamara didn't get what she wanted. He said he wanted to make her see that she could be replaced just like that." He snapped his fingers. "So he went after Morgan. Really turned on the charm."

He was silent for a few seconds. "Sean knew how I felt about her. He knew I'd asked her out. But he went after her anyway. He brought her to the house. He made out with her on the couch while I was sitting right there watching TV with them. I could see she was embarrassed, but . . ."

Mr. Charm, I thought.

"When I went to the arena to pick Sean up, I saw that kid, Billy, leaving. I went inside and I saw Sean on the ice.

I held my breath. What he said next could make all the difference.

"I asked him what Billy had been doing there," Colin said.

I exhaled. Colin had spoken to Sean. That meant that Sean was still alive after Billy left.

"What did he say?" I asked.

"He said Billy had come to beg him to leave Morgan alone. Sean just laughed. He said, 'For that, I think I'll keep her for a few more weeks.' He didn't care about her. He just cared about making Billy and Tamara miserable."

"Then what happened?" I said.

"Then I told him what I'd heard."

"Heard?"

"Some of the guys on the team told me that Sean was going to blow off college. I asked him about it."

"And?"

"He made a promise to our mom. Kevin and I—we never had the grades. Mom was really disappointed. But Sean promised. He was smart, and he promised."

I didn't say anything.

"Our mother drove us to all of our practices. She had to get up at five in the morning to make us breakfast and get us to the arena on time, but she never complained. After my dad took off, she had to make a lot of sacrifices to make sure we had the equipment we needed. And the only thing she wanted in return—the only thing—was for Sean to get an education."

"Maybe he thought he didn't need one," I said quietly.

"A promise is a promise," Colin said. "He had talent on the ice. He could have done okay in school, too, if he'd tried. But he thought he didn't have to. Sean was one of those guys who didn't realize how lucky he was.

He was going to have it all. He could have been nice to people. But instead he just used them."

"Did you show him the letter?"

"He was the only person who knew I had that doctor's appointment that day. You think he even asked me how it went?"

"Did you tell him?" I asked.

He nodded.

"What did he say?"

Colin stared out over the water and the park far below us.

"He said I would never have made it anyway. He said I was too much like Dad—all muscle and no skill."

"Is that when you—?"

"Three concussions," he said. "All of them from watching Sean's back. And that's all he could say to me? I lost it. I just lost it."

I remembered how his temper had raged out of control when he found out that Jon had tampered with Sean's helmet—and he hadn't made that discovery until after Sean was dead.

"Why did you cover up his face, Colin?"

"He was my brother. And I knew if I didn't bring him home, my mom would eventually go looking for him."

And she had. Sean's mother had been the one to find him.

"You knew where Billy lived," I said. "You followed him home from your house after he spied on Sean and Morgan. You threw the weapon into his yard, didn't you?"

"I couldn't face her," Colin said, his voice choked with anguish. "I couldn't face my mom. The idea of her looking at me and knowing what I'd done. And after what happened in the schoolyard . . ."

His hand shot out. I recoiled against the car door. But it wasn't me he was after. It was the door handle. He pushed the door open.

"Get out," he said. "Tell my mom I'm sorry. Tell her—tell her I love her. Tell her I loved Sean. Just, please, don't tell her the other stuff."

"Why don't you tell her yourself, Colin?" I said.

But he wasn't listening to me. He was staring straight ahead, through the windshield and out over the water. He turned the key in the ignition.

"Get out," he said. He released the parking brake and gunned the engine. He stared out at the open space ahead. What was he going to do?

"Colin—"

"Get out!"

I closed the car door and settled into my seat.

"She's your mother, Colin. She loves you."

He gripped the steering wheel. "Get out of the car."

"Turn off the engine, Colin."

He stared straight ahead.

"Please, Colin?"

Nothing.

I reached over, turned the key, yanked it from the ignition, and threw it out of the car.

Colin turned. I thought he was going to hit me, but he didn't. Instead, he slumped forward over the steering wheel, his shoulders shaking. He made a terrible sound. He was sobbing.

I groped on the floor of the car until I found my cell phone, and I punched in my dad's number.

CHAPTER **SIXTEEN**

"I don't get it," I said to Morgan the next morning. She had called me from the restaurant on the ground floor of my dad's building and asked me to come downstairs. I found her fretting over a latte. She begged me to go with her to Billy's house. "You've already talked to him on the phone. And you've known him practically your whole life. What are you so nervous about?"

"I dumped him," she said. "I yelled at him. I said all kinds of mean things about him. I treated him worse than anyone, and he still wanted to see me and talk to me and have my picture with him. Do you want me to go on?"

"But he already told you he still loves you."

"I know," she said. "But . . . I'd just feel better if you came with me. Please, Robyn?"

I said okay. Besides, I wanted to see Billy, too.

His mother answered the door. She beamed at Morgan. She frowned at me.

"Robyn, your face—"

"It looks worse than it feels," I told her. That was an understatement. I had tried to cover the bruises with concealer, but that just made my face look pale and lumpy. Without any makeup on, the whole side of my face looked like some crazy Picasso painting, all red and black and blue.

"I'm fine," I told her. "Really."

She looked doubtful but stepped aside to let us in. We found Billy seated at the kitchen table, which looked as if it had been set for a buffet for a dozen people. It was crowded with salads, casseroles, stir-fries, breads, juices—all of it one hundred percent vegan—and Billy was chowing down like there was no tomorrow. He stopped chewing when we walked into the room. His eyes went to Morgan first. He looked at her the way a kid looks when he's finally presented with the pony or the puppy that he's always wanted. Then, reluctantly— but I understood—he turned to me.

"What happened to you?" he said.

"I walked into a fist."

"Someone hit you?"

I told him what had happened at the arena and then said the same thing I had just said to his mother: "But I'm fine."

He smiled at me, turned back to Morgan, and invited us to sit down. "You hungry?" he said, reaching for what looked like some kind of tofu wrap. "My mom bought enough food to feed an army."

"How are you doing, Billy?" I said.

"It was great to walk out of that place. It was even better to be in my own bed last night. But it took me a long time to get to sleep. I kept thinking that maybe someone was playing a trick on me, that maybe the cops were going to come back and arrest me again and put me back inside there."

"Colin confessed," I said. "You don't have to worry about anything now, Billy."

"Thanks to you and Morgan. I know my parents believed me. But you and Morgan were the only people who did anything about it. You were the only ones who were in my corner the whole time."

I glanced at Morgan. She was looking down at a bowl of tabbouleh.

"Morgan?" Billy said softly. He reached across the table for her hand, which looked like my cue to get out of there. As I stood up, I noticed that Morgan was still staring at the salad.

"Morgan, what's wrong?" Billy said.

When she finally looked up, there were tears in her eyes. "I love you, Billy," she said.

"I love you too," Billy said. He reached for her again, but again she refused to take his hand.

"And I'm sorry I doubted you, too," she said.

"It's okay," Billy said. "I went kind of crazy when we broke up. I know I was being a pain. I knew it even when

I was doing it—I don't blame you for being mad at me. I wished you'd come to see me, but I understand. I mean, you knew him, and I guess you liked him."

"I was an idiot," Morgan said. "Sean was nothing like you, Billy. Not even close."

"You know what?" Billy said. "Let's not talk about him ever again. The important thing is that you were on my side. You believed in me."

A tear trickled down Morgan's cheek. "No, Billy," she said in a barely audible whisper, "I didn't."

Billy looked slightly baffled. "What do you mean?"

"Morgan," I said. But it was too late.

"I thought it was you," she said. "I'm sorry, Billy. But I really thought you did it. I know how stupid that was. You would never do anything like that. But—"

She stopped when she saw the look on his face. His mouth was slightly open, his head tilted to one side. If he was breathing, I couldn't tell. He looked like someone who had just been stabbed through the heart.

"I love you, Billy," Morgan said again. She was crying now. "I'm sorry I doubted you. I'm sorry for what I said."

Billy stood up and stepped away from the table. "I think you should leave," he said.

Then he turned and walked out of the kitchen. I heard his footsteps as he climbed the stairs to his room.

Billy's mother came into the kitchen to see what was going on. She looked at Morgan. Morgan wiped at her tears with the palms of her hands.

"He's tired," Billy's mother said. "I don't think he slept well in there. I know he didn't eat well. It's going to take some time for him to readjust."

Morgan stumbled to her feet. I followed her out of the house.

"You didn't have to tell him," I said.

"Yes, I did," Morgan said. "I was awful to him. I couldn't let him think something that wasn't true. I couldn't let him love me under false pretenses." More tears trickled down her cheeks. "I guess I don't have to worry about that anymore. I never should have broken up with him. I never should have gone with Sean."

I couldn't think of anything to say.

.   .   .

I was sitting in the window at my dad's place, watching for my mother's car. I had called her and told her that I'd had a slight accident and that my face was sort of bruised. My dad, who was on his way out when I was making the call, shook his head.

"You're just postponing the inevitable," he said.

He was right. But I knew my mother pretty well. If I told her over the phone exactly what had happened, she would make it out to be far worse. But if she could see me for herself, she would eventually realize that although my face looked terrible, I was basically all right.

"Make sure you tell her that I had nothing to do with it," my dad had said before he left.

I was just about to call Morgan to see how she was doing when someone knocked on the door. Because no one had buzzed first to be admitted into the building, I figured it had to be one of the tenants from the second floor. I went to the door and peeked through the peephole.

Nick.

My heart raced as I opened the door. "You just missed him," I said. "And he won't be back until late."

"I know," Nick said. "I heard him go out."

He stood out in the hall, looking right at me with his purple-blue eyes. He was lean and muscular in his black skinny jeans and a black T-shirt with a well-worn leather jacket over it.

"Are you really finished with that guy, Robyn?" he said.

"You mean Ben?"

He nodded.

"Yeah, I really am."

"How come? He didn't treat you bad, did he?"

I shook my head. "He's nice," I said. "But—"

"But what?"

I met his eyes and remembered all the times he had held me close. I remembered how warm I used to feel when he wrapped his arms tightly around me.

"But he's not you. I missed you, Nick."

He took a step closer to me, forcing me to tip my head up to keep looking at him.

"I missed you, too."

My phone rang. Nick glanced at it. So did I.

"It's my mother," I said. I held my phone to my ear.

"I'm right downstairs," she said. "And I'm in a hurry, Robyn. So—"

"I'll be right there, Mom."

I ended the call and looked at Nick.

"I have to go."

"That's okay. I know where to find you."

Then he kissed me. Lightly. Gently. Sweetly. So sweetly that all I wanted to do was wrap myself around him forever and ever.

"Nick—"

"I'll call you tomorrow," he said. "I promise."

After my mom had seen my face, after she had freaked out, and after I had finally calmed her down again and she'd started the car and pulled out into traffic, she glanced at me and said, "What on earth are you smiling about?"

"Nothing," I said.

.   .   .

Billy didn't come back to school until Wednesday. I spotted him as soon as I got off the bus. He was standing in front of the school with Dennis Hanson. Dennis was talking, but he wasn't looking directly at Billy. Billy was nodding. He looked much better than he had the last time I'd seen him. He still looked thin and tired, but when he saw me and smiled, he looked like the Billy I had always known.

Then he looked beyond me.

Morgan was coming up the street. She stopped in her tracks when she saw Billy.

"I'll be right back," Billy said to Dennis. He walked past me to Morgan and stood in front of her for a moment. Neither of them said anything. Then Billy put out his arms and Morgan walked into them and they just stood there, clinging to each other. They didn't seem to care that everyone was looking at them. Even Dennis.

CHECK OUT THE NEXT BOOK IN THE
ROBYN HUNTER MYSTERIES SERIES:

IN TOO
DEEP

A creepy-crawly feeling crept down my spine. I glanced at the gas gauge.
I had a quarter tank left. That would be enough to get back to town, right?
Increasingly panicky, I groped for my phone. I would call Morgan and
do my best to describe where I was. Something darted across the road.
A deer? I swerved to avoid hitting it. And went off the road into the ditch.

#1 Last Chance

Robyn's scared of dogs—but she agrees to spend time at an animal shelter anyway. Robyn learns that many juvenile offenders also volunteer at the shelter—including Nick D'Angelo. Nick has a talent for troublemaking, but after his latest arrest, Robyn suspects that he might be innocent. And she sets out to prove it . . .

#2 You Can Run

Trisha Hanover has run away from home before. But this time, she hasn't come back. To make matters worse, Robyn blew up at Trisha the same morning she disappeared. Now Robyn feels responsible, and she decides to track Trisha down . . .

#3 Nothing to Lose

Robyn is excited to hang out with Nick after weeks apart. She's sure he has reformed—until she notices suspicious behavior during their trip to Chinatown. Turns out Nick's been doing favors for dangerous people. Robyn urges him to stop, but the situation might be out of her control—and Nick's . . .

#4 Out of the Cold

Robyn's friend Billy drags her into volunteering at a homeless shelter. When one of the shelter's regulars freezes to death on a harsh winter night, Robyn wonders if she could've prevented it. She sets out to find about more about the man's past, and discovers unexpected danger in the process . . .

#5 *Shadow of Doubt*

Robyn's new substitute teacher Ms. Denholm is cool, pretty, and possibly the target of a stalker. When Denholm receives a threatening package, Robyn wonders who's responsible. But Robyn has a mystery of her own to worry about: What's with the muddled phone message she receives from her missing ex-boyfriend Nick?

#6 *Nowhere to Turn*

Robyn has sworn that she's over Nick. But when she hears he needs help, she's too curious about why he went missing to say no. Nick has been arrested again, and the evidence doesn't lean in his favor. When Robyn investigates, she discovers a situation more complicated than the police had thought—and more deadly . . .

#7 *Change of Heart*

Robyn's best friend Billy has been a mess ever since her other best friend Morgan dumped him. To make matters worse, Morgan started dating hockey star Sean Sloane right afterward. Billy is an animal rights activist—he wouldn't hurt a fly. But when Sean winds up dead, can Robyn prove Billy's innocence?

#8 In Too Deep

Robyn should be having the time of her life. She has a great summer job and a room in Morgan's lake house. But suddenly Nick appears in town—on a mission. He promised a friend he'd investigate a local suicide. Did Alex Richmond drown himself? Or was he killed because he knew too much?

#9 At the Edge

Robyn just wants to spend time with Nick, but he's always busy. Morgan thinks James Derrick, a hot transfer student, could take Nick off her mind. But James has problems of his own. When Robyn realizes she and James share a hidden connection, she starts to dig deeper. But is she digging her own grave?

ABOUT THE AUTHOR

Norah McClintock is the author of several mystery series for teenagers and a five-time winner of the Crime Writers of Canada's Arthur Ellis Award for Best Juvenile Crime Novel. McClintock was born and raised in Montreal, Quebec. She lives in Toronto with her husband and children.